Can artificial life be as real as
biological life?

Written by
Blaski

CINEMATIC
PUBLISHERS

UNITED WORLDS by Blaski

A cinematic science-fiction experience.

First edition, February 2026.

Published in the United States by Cinematic Publishers.

ISBN: 979-8-9939888-0-1

Cover design, book design, and illustrations by Lucila Duloup

The Library of Congress has cataloged this edition as follows:

Name: Blaski, author.

Title: United Worlds

Description: First United States edition.

For information or rights inquiries, contact:

cinematicpublishers@gmail.com

CINEMATIC
PUBLISHERS

Dedicated to Lula Duloup, my wife,
whose contributions and support
made this book possible.

CONTENT

ACT 1

ACT 2   PART 1

Before we begin...

This is a screenplay with elements of a novel, written for science fiction fans who may have never read a screenplay before.

I wrote this to feel cinematic. It's fast-paced, visual, and driven by action and dialogue. When you read it, you'll see *your* movie.

The inspiration for this story came from using virtual reality during the pandemic. While in lockdown, I traveled to different worlds and was blown away. If VR feels this real now, what happens when the technology evolves? What happens when it becomes indistinguishable from the physical world?

Can virtual reality be as real as physical reality? And down the rabbit hole I went. Can an uploaded mind without a body still be human? Can artificial life be as real as biological life?

These are the questions at the heart of this story.

All right. Thanks for reading, and enjoy the show!

Artificial life isn't real life

to save the real, I dive into the lie,
and trade my soul before I let her die.
—Bowen Huxley

Chapter 1
Hooked to this ilusion

22 min read

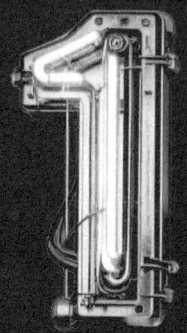

In the black void, reddish-orange particles collide again and again, at insane speeds, releasing bursts of white-hot energy.

As the chaos intensifies, waves of bluish-white plasma form and twist together into a blue-purple vortex.

From within it, an artificial sun roars to life, caged inside a machine.

The blinding blue-purple light grows, expanding until it floods everything.

INTERIOR NUCLEAR FUSION POWER PLANT - DUSK

Blue-purple light leaks through the seams of a massive, doughnut-shaped fusion reactor, a monument built to contain a raging star. The air vibrates with a low, unending hum, as if the machine itself were breathing.

The futuristic machine gleams against the industrial walls, the concrete scarred and the paint flaking away. All the money poured into tech, while the building rots around it.

At a workbench cluttered with tools, BOWEN HUXLEY repairs a small spider-like robot with obsessive focus. He is in his early 20s, undernourished, with a silver ring in his nose. He sweeps his messy black hair back, revealing green eyes behind safety goggles, his gaze too intense for his age.

He touches invisible things in the air as he works on the robot, looking like a crazy person who sees things that aren't there.

FROM BOWEN'S POINT OF VIEW (he sees in black & white): Through Bowen's eyes, virtual objects float around the robot, offering suggestions and live reports to assist with his job, projected by his Augmented Reality goggles.

BOWEN

All set. Finish your rounds, bud.

He sets the robot down, and it crawls across the floor, up the reactor's side, sensors flickering as it runs its checks.

Bowen wipes the grease from his hands onto his

mechanic's jumpsuit. Two worn patches are stitched to his chest, one reading *Robotics Engineer*, the other *Bowen*. Once most of the grease is off, he massages his rough, scabbed palms with his thumbs, trying to ease the dull ache left by another long day. Too many extra shifts. Always.

FROM BOWEN'S POV (B&W): A virtual countdown grows larger, sliding into the center of his vision.

> 5...
>
> 4...
>
> 3...
>
> 2...
>
> 1...

The timer freezes at 1, then jumps, adding six more hours to his shift.

BOWEN

Tsk. C'mon!

A violent sigh escapes him. He puts on his headphones, rock music pouring in, and pulls up a virtual screen. His fingers fly as he hacks into the power plant's system, coding inhumanly fast, with the speed of someone who's done this a thousand times.

FROM BOWEN'S POV (B&W): The countdown accelerates.

> 3...
>
> 2...

1...

SHIFT COMPLETE

As he lowers the goggles to his neck, the virtual objects vanish, red marks ringing his eyes from wearing them all day.

And off he goes, running across the power plant like a prisoner breaking free.

EXTERIOR POWER PLANT - DUSK

An isolated power plant sits high in the mountains, surrounded by dense autumn forest blazing with color. Below, the deep blue waters of Lake Tahoe reflect the warm oranges of the sky.

Bowen comes out the employee entrance with a conquering smile and hops on a rusty green bike.

He speeds downhill, passing a yellow diamond-shaped sign with the silhouette of a bear and her cub.

EXT. MAIN STREET - CONTINUOUS

Bowen bikes past a welcome sign: "Homewood: Living Real, Loving Real."

It's a small mountain community where everyone knows each other, a humble little town where life moves with a slow, steady pulse.

A traffic sign warns: HUMAN-DRIVEN CARS NEXT 10 MILES.

The street hugs the lake, buried under a carpet of golden leaves. Local businesses sit with a first-row view of the mountains and water. A bohemian boutique, an astrology reading shop, a soul therapy center, a store selling herbs and aromatherapy.

Outside the Black Bear Diner, a NO ROBOTS ALLOWED sign hangs in the window. A young hippie waitress sweeps leaves, her long brown hair draping past a flower headband and her arms stacked with multicolored bracelets. She stops, her eyes narrowing as Bowen rides by. *Technofreak.*

The hardware store has a prominent banner: HANDMADE REPAIRS ONLY. The owner leans in the doorway, smoking, watching Bowen with pure hate, like he's the enemy.

Nearby, a black crow pecks at roadkill, taking flight as Bowen pedals past. He lets go of the handlebars, arms spread like wings, wishing he could just lift off and fly with it.

He races past closed shops with FOR RENT signs and a burnt-down store with a bullet-riddled sign: "Links to the United Worlds by the Hour." In the ashes, a protest sign stands: LIFE IS SACRED, NOT ARTIFICIAL.

Two bearded men in their 30s, fly rods in hand, scowl at Bowen. Everyone knows he works with robots, and they hate him for it.

He rides past a Christian church, its message board reading: ARTIFICIAL WORLDS CANNOT SAVE YOUR SOUL.

Turning into an alley, he meets the message painted in bold letters on the wall: WE CHOOSE TO LIVE IN GOD'S REALITY.

EXT. FOREST - CONTINUOUS

Bowen bikes past a wooden shelter designed for observing animals.

A few moments later, the path leads to an open-air workshop. A camouflage tarp stretches overhead like a makeshift ceiling, protecting piles of machines that don't exist anywhere else.

From a table buried under tools and robot parts, he grabs a homemade virtual reality (VR) headset. It's an assembly of special lenses, sensors, and chips, all topped with a brain-computer-interface disc shaped like a Jewish skullcap.

Carefully, he places the VR headset inside his vintage leather backpack.

EXT. BOWEN'S HOUSE - NIGHT

A humble cabin glows under camping string lights, tucked so deep into the trees it seems one with nature. In the yard, a sign reads: KEEP HOMEWOOD REAL.

FROM BOWEN'S POV (B&W): Stripped of color, the charming cabin looks haunted and precarious. He takes the headphones off, the rock music fading.

He throws his bike beside a beaten-up futuristic van

wrapped in colorful flower graphics and religious stickers. One, shaped like a heart, reads: "God is great." A larger one on the rear window declares: "Jesus is my savior."

INT. BOWEN'S HOUSE - CONTINUOUS

Bowen enters, collapsing into a squeaky chair. The place is a mess, piles of books, clothes, and boxes scattered everywhere. It's so small that everything is just a few steps away, the kind of space that makes you feel claustrophobic.

BOWEN

Mom, I'm home.

He waits for an answer, worried, as he takes off his work boots and rubs his feet, his socks mismatched and full of holes.

Feeling the cold, he feeds a heavy log to the dying fire. Above the fireplace, black block letters spell FAITH beneath a large wooden cross nailed to the wall.

BOWEN

Mom?

(waits, no answer)

Mom? You okay?

He hears a low, prolonged groan and rushes to the bathroom, afraid of what he will find.

ABI, 67, a loving but strict hippie with long gray hair, lies on the wooden floor, too weak to get up. She looks like she has been there for hours.

BOWEN

Jesus, Mom. You okay?

He lifts her up – she feels light, too light – and helps her out of the bathroom. She has to duck to clear the doorframe, her legs shaking as she clings to him. She is as big as a grizzly bear on two legs, but sickness has stripped her strength.

Clearly, Bowen takes after his father more than his mother, who looks nothing like him, as she is of Japanese descent.

BOWEN

How are you feeling?

She offers a small, uncertain smile, dark circles framing her swollen eyes. She scratches her skin too much.

ABI

(extremely surprised)

You shaved.

He looks down, forcing a smile, and helps her onto the stained couch. He wraps her in a blanket, rubbing her arms and back, trying to warm her skin, cold as ice.

ABI

(giving him a present)

Happy birthday, Bowie.

It's a picture of a futuristic blue fishing boat covered in

snow, sitting in a lonely parking lot in the woods. It's framed with twigs, leaves, and tiny pinecones.

>   ABI
>
> I framed the photo you took last winter.
> For your room. You like it?

>   BOWEN
>
> Look at that.
>   (hugs her and kisses her)
> I love it. Thanks, Mom.

He walks into the bathroom to wash his hands, leaving the door open.

>   ABI
>
> Why do you like that picture so much?
> Don't get me wrong, I like it. But why is
> it your favorite?

>   BOWEN
>
> Boats are meant to be in the water. But
> that one's stuck out there, abandoned,
> waiting in a parking lot, covered in snow.
>   (shrugs)
> Don't know. It's kinda poetic.

Bowen takes a box of medication from the fridge and sits beside her. She opens the coffee-table drawer, laying out a pill organizer and alcohol swabs over a half-finished jigsaw puzzle. The daily ritual. From the box, he pulls out a pen-injector, uncaps it, and twists a fresh needle onto the tip. Abi lifts her white nightgown, revealing a thin, bruised thigh. Bowen cleans the spot with an alcohol swab, pinches her skin, barely anything to hold, and injects the medication. He catches her wincing and presses his lips together, feeling a sorrow that doesn't fade with time.

Bowen unscrews the needle and throws it inside a small red bin next to the fridge. When he turns back toward the kitchen sink, he is disappointed to see a dish with black ants crawling over melted cheese.

BOWEN
Mom. Grilled cheese? Again? Really?

He rinses them away and holds up the dish. She gives a tight-lipped smile, her eyes saying, *I couldn't help myself.*

ABI
It was just a little bit, Bowie. I was hungry.
It doesn't hurt.

BOWEN
It does hurt. It can kill you. And you
know that. The doctor couldn't have
been more clear: no cheese. Not even
once. I don't...

Bowen turns to clean the dish, shaking his head.

Unbelievable. He scrubs with all his strength at the melted cheese that won't budge, fused to the plate, like a bad dream that won't go away.

He pauses, staring at it, exhausted. Never a minute to rest. He tries again, this time with a steel wool scrubber.

> BOWEN
> You know, I wish you'd let me build a
> robot to help us around the house.

> ABI
> Again with that? Don't be so stubborn,
> son.

She swallows a pill with a sip of water, one of many she takes throughout the day.

> ABI
> It's not natural. Look, it's bad enough
> you work with robots, okay? I don't want
> anything artificial in this house.

He reaches for the switch and flips the lights off.

> ABI
> Hey!

> BOWEN
> (turning the lights back on)
> You said: no artificial things.

ABI

You always wanna debate, don't you?

He gets to work on dinner, preparing chicken and rice, the only dish they have eaten since she was last hospitalized.

ABI

You know, some neighbors came by today and asked if I needed anything. Did you ask 'em to?

(off his busted expression)

Bowen! I already feel guilty having you take care of me.

BOWEN

It's fine. They just wanna help.

He turns his back to her, stirring the chicken and rice while watching her reflection in the dark window glass. His eyes move from side to side, the way someone does when they are about to say something delicate.

BOWEN

You know what this old guy at work told me? He said robotics engineers used to make good money. Can you believe that? Don't know what happened, but it pisses me off that I can't save enough for your treatment, you know?

ABI

My treatment? What treatment?

BOWEN

So, it's very expensive but – and please,
just hear me out – they can use your cells
to... uh, create a bioengineered kidney.

Thunder roars. Heavy rain starts pouring down.

She hobbles to the kitchen table, her slippers scraping
across the wooden floor.

ABI

Right... But you know me, Bowie. An
artificial kidney? You crazy?

BOWEN

Mom, you don't get it. It's a kidney
genetically identical to the one you had
before.

ABI

It's not natural. And can you imagine
what people would say? They'd kick me
out of church.

BOWEN

If you don't, you'll die.

She freezes, pondering those words, a declaration she

didn't expect from her son.

> BOWEN
>
> I'm sorry to say it like this, Mom, but...
> you don't have much time.

> ABI
>
> Why're we even discussing this? Didn't
> you say it's expensive?

He stays silent, but his expression falters. She studies his face, sensing he is holding something back.

> ABI
>
> What is it?

> BOWEN
>
> Uh, I... Well, that's actually what... I, uh,
> got an interview for a security engineer
> position. The pay's really good, you
> know? In a few months, I could get the
> money.

He sets a pot on the floor to catch the rainwater leaking from the roof. *Plink, plink, plink.*

> BOWEN
>
> In this economy, you know, it's really
> hard to get an interview for this type
> of work. Especially without formal
> education.

(pause)

But I'll pull it off, Mom. You'll see. I've been studying day and night in my free time, practicing with this...

He grabs his backpack, and the moment he takes out the VR headset, a sharp gasp escapes her lips. She stares at it in horror, clutching her crucifix necklace, her narrow black eyes going wide.

ABI

What in God's name are you doing with that old junk? You know it's forbidden. Who gave you that?

BOWEN

...Uh, I... built it. But, it doesn't send signals to my brain. So I can't fully immerse in virtual reality. And, uh, well, for this job, I need all the sensory experiences of the real world. So, you know, I need a lifepod capsule.

ABI

Wait. Hold on, hold on. You're saying this job is in the United Worlds?

He nods, looking away, knowing it's a sensitive topic. The shock hits her hard. Her breath catches in her throat, turning into a ragged wheeze as she struggles to inhale. He rushes to her side, rubbing her back to soothe her. She clutches the crucifix tighter, squeezing strength out of it, forcing a gulp of air into her lungs until she finds her voice.

ABI

Oh my God. I can't believe this.

BOWEN
(hugging her from behind)
I'm leaving tomorrow, Mom.

ABI

Tomorrow?!

She breaks his hold, twisting around to face him. *That can't be right.* He leans down, grabbing her hands to steady her.

ABI
Bowie, I know you wanna do this for me,
okay? But don't. Seriously. Artificial life
isn't real life.

BOWEN
I know, Mom. It's not like I wanna live
in a coffin like the rest of the world. And
maybe I don't even get the job.
(pause)
But if I do, it will be just 'till I save enough

for the treatment, okay?

ABI

But it's dangerous. Everyone's hooked to this... illusion like junkies. It's so addictive they prefer to live in that fake world built –

BOWEN
(interrupting)
Built by corrupt people instead of this one created by God. Yes, yes, I know. I feel sorry for them. But don't worry. You know me. I'm not gonna waste my life on something that's not real. I'll save enough money for the treatment and come back.
(off her worried expression)
You don't have to worry about anything. I'll send money every week and have someone take care of you. And the neighbors will help out 'till I get my first paycheck. That's why they came today.

ABI
You-you told them? You told them you're going to the United Worlds?

BOWEN

I told them a job somewhere else. Don't
worry. I left that part out.

(pause)

Mom, look at me. You'll be fine.

ABI

You think I'm worried about me? I'm
worried about you. If something happens
to you? Huh? The United Worlds is an
independent country with its own rules.
It's not a game. People die there! Their
soldiers... They're ruthless. You got no
idea. Trust me.

(pause)

You know what happens when they
shoot people in the United Worlds,
right? They die for real. Lifepods kill
their brains. No! I-I-I–

(deep breath)

No. You can't be so stubborn, son. The
United Worlds is a sin against everything
we believe in.

He looks down, ashamed, feeling her disappointment.
Again. She grabs his hands and offers a weak smile, thinking
she's finally won the argument.

BOWEN

So I should do nothing and let you die?

Her face softens as her gaze drifts away, realizing the burden she has placed on him, far heavier than she ever imagined.

Heavy rain hammers the tin roof, drowning out the silence.

BOWEN

I want you to be healthy, okay? Enjoy life again. Go on hikes. We used to go hiking every week. Remember that day? The day a family of deer ran past us? They were so close we felt the ground shaking. It was magical.

(pause)

With a bioengineered kidney you'll need no more medication. No more depending on others. Don't you want that?

She'd like that, but this goes against their values and beliefs. Their souls would rot in hell if they did this.

* * *

Bowen lies cramped on a narrow, short mattress, wrapped in dusty covers. Even with his knees tucked, the bed is too small for him. He stares through the window at the raging storm, wide-eyed and pensive, the wind howling against the thin walls.

A cough echoes down the hall.

He gets up and goes to her bedroom, gently elevating her head with extra pillows so she can sleep upright.

ABI

Can you get me some water?

BOWEN

But you already drank two cups today.

ABI

Please, Bowie. My mouth is dry as a desert. It's the medication...

BOWEN

But just a sip, okay? The doctor said more than two cups is dangerous.

In the kitchen, he pours water into a glass, catching his reflection in the window. Who will do all this when he's gone?

Back in Abi's bedroom, he helps her take a sip, and kisses her goodnight.

EXT. BOWEN'S HOUSE - DAWN

Wet autumn leaves cling to tree branches. A droplet strikes a dark purple leaf, knocking it loose. Birds chirp softly, their songs threading through the cold morning mist.

Bowen and Abi stand in the doorway of the small cabin, holding each other in a long, quiet hug. She towers over him, her massive frame making his six-foot-three height look small. They stand bathed in the soft golden glow of sunlight filtering through the woods, the thick fog turning the light into long, heavy beams.

> BOWEN
>
> I'm gonna miss you.

> ABI
>
> (gripping his arm)
> Don't go, Bowie. Stay. Please. I'll do better. I'll take better care of myself. No more cheese, I swear.

> BOWEN
>
> Good. That's great. But it's not enough. I'm sorry, Mom, but there's no other way. You need a new kidney. And you need it now.

She knows he's right, and her son is so stubborn there's nothing she can say that will make him stay.

> ABI
>
> (adjusting his beanie)
> Just... don't let that place change you,

okay? You've got a beautiful soul. And
stay outta trouble, you hear me?

He picks up his backpack and duffel bag. They pull into
another hug, the kind where neither wants to be the first to
let go.

> ABI
> Just be careful, okay? Promise me. I
> know you're a man now, but to me you'll
> always be my Bo-Bo.

> BOWEN
> (rolling his eyes)
> Mom, c'mon. Stop.

> ABI
> Well, I'm sorry. But it's the truth.
> (grabs his face)
> And whatever happens, I'll be here. This
> will always be your home.

> BOWEN
> I'll let you know when I get there. I'll send
> you messages through Pastor Lucas.

Abi's eyes shine, ready to cry, already feeling the
emptiness he is leaving behind.

> BOWEN
>
> Hey, don't worry. Hey. I'll visit as soon as
> I can, okay? I promise.
>
> (hugs her again)
>
> Love you.

> ABI
>
> I love you too, son.

Bowen takes one last look at his mother, terrified to leave her alone. But there is no other way. He turns and walks away, dodging puddles along the muddy road, desperate to return soon with good news.

As he puts his headphones on, electronic music floods in, a blend of nostalgia and discovery that carries him forward, downhill.

She makes the sign of the cross and, clinging to her crucifix necklace, shuts her eyes tight to pray, the cold morning air turning her whispers into mist.

INT. BUS - MORNING

Bowen rides a futuristic bus with no driver. Across from him, an elderly woman sits buried under more bags than she can carry, her face mapped with deep, exhausted wrinkles. She wears a black cap with "I love Jesus" stuck to the brim and a Bible patch stitched to the side. She meets Bowen's gaze and shakes her head in disapproval.

Bowen shifts in his seat, turning away. He stares at the calm blue lake that mirrors the world he's never left before. His fingers tighten on the edge of the seat, anxiety creeping in as he heads into the unknown.

Chapter 2
Humans and uploads don't mix

28 min read

Previously...

Bowen is a stubborn tech genius living in a small mountain town that rejects technology. His mother is dying, and they can't afford the treatment.

He gets a job interview that could pay enough to save her. The catch is... the job is in the United Worlds, an independent country that exists inside virtual reality. To them, the United Worlds is a deadly sin, an ungodly place that isn't real and hooks people with illusions, wasting their lives.

But Bowen has no choice. He leaves home, heading into the world he hates to save the person he loves.

EXT. SAN FRANCISCO CITY - DUSK

The red Golden Gate Bridge floats in the fog.

As the mist clears, a futuristic San Francisco comes into view. Towers glow with dynamic OLED art and neon lights. Drones fly in and out of beehive-shaped buildings.

Massive sea walls protect the city from flooding. On them, painted in bold letters: ESCAPE THE FAKE, JOIN THE REAL.

Humanoid and mechanical robots construct a building, some with their metal frames vandalized with graffiti.

FROM A DRONE'S POV: Bowen looks up, stunned by the city's architecture. He has never seen buildings this tall.

The drone scans his face. "BOWEN HUXLEY // ROBOTICS ENGINEER @ NUCLEAR FUSION POWER PLANT - LAKE TAHOE // SOCIAL SCORE: 62.3 (LOW RISK)."

FROM BOWEN'S POV (B&W): People with crazy hair and filthy clothes lie passed out on the sidewalks, tents crowding the curb, trash piled everywhere. Robots don't clean this part of the city anymore.

A young man presses a patch of magenta liquid to his arm. The ink crawls under his skin like living circuits, lighting up briefly before dissolving into the blood. His body softens, his head tilting back as the tension drains away. A faint smile lingers.

Many take that drug. Addicts are easy to spot because they glow all the time, their veins lit like neon, burned in place from too many hits.

An OLED video poster features RHEA, looking barely out of her teens, with striking red-and-white hair. Her face is covered in freckles, her green eyes burning with a fire she can't fully hide.

RHEA (ON POSTER)

Power belongs to the people. Not to politicians or the rich. That's why, in the United Worlds, citizens propose laws, and everyone has the right to vote on them. We use Tores, our digital token that keeps your vote secure and anonymous. So get your Tore today, become a citizen, and help shape the future. Join the United Worlds.

The video poster sits inside a rusted shopping cart pushed by a homeless man. His weathered face is tattooed with geometric shapes in black, blue, and red, a pattern designed to confuse facial recognition tech.

As the shopping cart rattles past, it reveals a stylish endless building wrapped in colorful tiles, each one shaped like a W.

INT. UNITED WORLDS PORT - CONTINUOUS

A grand lobby stretches beneath a vaulted glass ceiling that seems miles away. Tiers of balconies spiral upward, vanishing into the height, lined with ironwork so delicate it looks like art. Elegant and sharp. It makes a 5-star hotel look like a motel.

The United Worlds banner hangs in a tall drape, its dark blue and black stripes running vertically. In the center, a white emblem made of six circles ringing one, with slices cut from the outer circles.

Two United Worlds soldiers stand guard in dark blue camouflage uniforms. High-tech helmets with reflective blue visors hide their eyes.

A SALESWOMAN in her 40s, whose fakeness is hard to miss, trains a junior salesman as they assist a wealthy family with two kids.

> SALESWOMAN
>
> Honestly, living in the United Worlds
> is better for the planet. Less pollution,
> less–

She pauses, struck by Bowen's rugged natural-fiber clothes, a stark contrast to their sleek outfits.

> SALESWOMAN
> (to Bowen)
> Don't make me call security.

The family stares. The mother turns her kids away. Caught off guard, Bowen stands hurt and speechless. He takes off his beanie and smooths his messy black hair, feeling out of place.

The saleswoman signals the soldiers, who march straight toward Bowen.

> BOWEN
>
> Uh, sorry, I wanna go to the United
> Worlds. This is a port, right?

> SALESWOMAN
> ...Right. Sure. You know our prices, right?

> BOWEN
> Yeh, no, I know. But I got a coupon.

He lifts his thumb. The saleswoman glares, then

reluctantly scans his finger with a portable device. As she reads Bowen's information, she wipes the sensor, just in case he has something contagious.

> SALESWOMAN
>
> Mhm. So after converting your US dollars to UW dollars... and even with your discount applied... you can only afford three days. And that's excluding expenses. You'll probably get a day or two, max.
>
> (patronizing tone)
>
> You sure about this?

He nods. She rolls her eyes, letting out a sharp sigh, then forces a smile to the family and mouths a silent "sorry."

Bowen follows the saleswoman down an endless hallway. The walls are alive with OLED screens projecting rare 3D images and animations, showing the evolution of VR technology in cool and weird designs.

INT. ROOM #2222 - CONTINUOUS

They enter a minimalist room bathed in blue and purple light.

Bowen is drawn to a lifepod, a high-tech enclosed capsule that stimulates the brain to be fully immersed in virtual reality. It stands reclined at a 45-degree angle, purple neon strips outlining its sleek design.

> SALESWOMAN
> (pointing to folding screens)
> Over there. Take your clothes off.

He walks behind the screens and begins to undress, eyeing the artificial glow that fills the room.

> BOWEN
> What's the deal with the lights?

> SALESWOMAN
> Helps with the transition back to the
> Offline. Useless, really. Nobody leaves
> these days.

> BOWEN
> But, uh, people can leave whenever they
> want, right?

> SALESWOMAN
> What do you think? You go to a terminal
> and go through customs. Like when you
> travel to another country.

Bowen lifts his eyebrows, surprised by her aggression. How would he know? He never went to the United Worlds. He never traveled to another country. Hell, he never even left Tahoe.

When he finishes putting on a high-end gown, he speeds to the lifepod, climbs in, and shuts the door. A rectangular smart-glass panel frames his face, his eyes wide and darting like a trapped animal, his rapid breath fogging the glass.

BOWEN
...What about going to the bathroom?

SALESWOMAN
Relax. No need to exit for that. These lifepods have everything you need. And more. Revolutionary life support system. You'll be fine.
(points to a device)
C'mon, put that on. I don't have all day.

He places a neurostimulator on his head. The dome is covered in rows of raised haptic nodes that rise to a central antenna. It resembles a futuristic Buddha's crown, as if its designers believed this technology could unlock a new kind of enlightenment.

She taps SCAN BRAIN on the pod's door, and a screen lights up on the surface. A 3D map of his brain forms in real-time, a glowing web of purple and red nodes connected by crimson lines.

BOWEN
...I don't think it's working.

SALESWOMAN

Give it a few seconds, will you? It's mapping your brain. Not making toast.
(whispering to herself)
Or whatever you *hippies* eat in your little commune.

BOWEN

Oh, shit. My nose ring. Should I –?

Before he can complete the question, a whooshing sound cuts him off, and the smart-glass panel polarizes, hiding his face behind it.

INT. UNITED WORLDS TERMINAL - NIGHT

A vast futuristic airport hums with movement. Bustling crowds flow beneath a tunnel-like ceiling glowing with magenta and orange neon strips, their colors reflecting across the glossy floor. A massive floating circle reads UNITED WORLDS at the top and TERMINAL at the bottom.

Everything looks real, indistinguishable from the physical world. Virtual reality at its finest.

Bowen stares in awe. He looks exactly the same, with his messy black hair and nose ring. His green eyes widen, taking in the vibrant colors for the first time. It's too much beauty to absorb. He blinks repeatedly, unable to trust his vision, as if he's discovering a new world.

The saleswoman materializes. She wears the same uniform, but she looks much younger and sexier than she did in the Offline. Beside her floats a mirror. Bowen stares into it, seeing himself in color, something unthinkable all his life. His smile trembles, overwhelmed by the miracle. He touches his reflection, as if the color might wash off. Tears roll down.

> BOWEN
>
> I-I... but how?
>
> (laughs)
>
> I've got this, uh, condition where I only see in black and white. But... I'm seeing colors! Actual colors!

He hugs her, then recoils, realizing he overstepped.

SALESWOMAN

...Yeah, you get all your senses here. Even
if you don't have them in the Offline.

(pause)

Okay, listen, we'll send you alerts when
it's time to exit, all right?

She and the mirror vanish before he can respond.

Bowen rubs his fingers together and laughs, marveling
at how real it feels. He squeezes his arms, finding the bones,
the muscles. Then pulls the hair on his arm, sensing the skin
stretch, and scratches the bluish veins beneath.

His eyes spark with an idea. Looking around to make sure
nobody is watching, he touches his dick. *Wow!* His eyes go
even wider. *Holy shit.*

A whisper from behind makes Bowen jump. He whips
around to find a PROFESSIONAL WOMAN in her 40s,
dressed in a white silk blouse with a neat low ponytail.
She leans in, whispering again. Whatever she is saying, it is
completely inaudible.

BOWEN

Sorry?

She shoots a paranoid look to both sides, ensuring no
one is following her.

PROFESSIONAL WOMAN

Do you struggle with bills?

BOWEN

What?

PROFESSIONAL WOMAN

Or health problems?

Bowen glares at her.

PROFESSIONAL WOMAN

Tired of paying a fortune for lifepods?
Say goodbye to your money problems
or health problems. Upload now. For a
fraction of the cost, I can upload you–

SECURITY

Hey!

She shoves a card into Bowen's hand and runs away. The
SECURITY GUY stops beside Bowen and snatches it.

BOWEN

Sorry. I don't want any trouble. I don't...
I don't know her.

SECURITY

Her?
(chuckles)
That's not a person.

> (laughs harder)
> It's an advertisement.

The guard walks away, laughing. Bowen shrinks into himself, staring at the floor, glancing around to make sure nobody saw that. He feels like a complete idiot.

* * *

As Bowen waits in line, a welcome video plays across the massive screens. Rhea appears, looking barely out of her teens with striking red-and-white hair, freckled face, and green eyes. Behind her hangs the United Worlds flag, its dark blue and black stripes running vertically.

> RHEA (ON VIDEO)
> Welcome to the United Worlds, the newest nation on Earth. Except... it isn't on Earth at all.
> (smiles)
> The United Worlds is the only country that exists purely in virtual reality. We perfected full immersion, making you feel and experience everything just as you would in the physical world. But here, the impossible is possible. That's why 6.6 billion people have already made it their home.

(pause)

The United Worlds is a sovereign, independent nation like no other. A nation where the people are the lawmakers. Any citizen can propose laws, and everyone can vote on them using Tores, our digital token that guarantees both equality and anonymity. One person, one Tore, one vote.

(pause)

And freedom doesn't stop there. We're a country where anyone can start a business, own their work, build a home, raise a family. A place where dreams belong to those who dare to make them.

(pause)

We hope you enjoy your stay. And thank you for visiting... the United Worlds.

An intimidating IMMIGRATION OFFICER shouts from his booth.

OFFICER

Next!

Bowen rushes over, nervous.

OFFICER

Bowen Huxley? Only three days?

Bowen chuckles. The officer waits for an answer, impatient.

> BOWEN
>
> Yeh, well... initially, sir. Uh, you see, that's what I can afford right now.
>
> (clears throat)
>
> But I have a job interview tomorrow. For a security engineer position, actually.

Bowen nods and smiles, proudly. The officer isn't impressed.

> BOWEN
>
> We'll be on the same side. You and me. Keeping the United Worlds safe. Safe from criminals.
>
> (gets nothing from him)
>
> That's what security engineers do, you know? Make sure hackers can't break in.

> OFFICER
>
> Mhm. So then you know. Break our laws, and we can punish you here or in your country. By entering, you're accepting the terms and conditions. You agree?
>
> (Bowen nods)
>
> I need to hear you say it.

BOWEN

Sorry, yeh, I agree. I acc–

The officer slams a button, dissolving Bowen.

INT. CLASSIC HOME - DAY

Bowen materializes in a sleek, minimalist living room.

A floating menu hovers in front of him showing home options. He taps PARADISE BEACH HOUSE and the place transforms into a cozy tropical haven of wood and sunlight, with a wide deck opening to an ocean view. The sound of waves filters in. He spreads his arms wide, catching the breeze against his skin, his face lit by a wide smile.

He turns to the menu and taps LAKE HOUSE. The world ripples, shifting into a glass-walled sanctuary floating above turquoise water while a flock of birds flies across the sky. But his eyes are already glued to the last option on the menu: SPACE STATION. As he taps it, everything fades.

INT. SPACE STATION

Bowen turns slowly, stunned, absorbing the impossible view.

The walls and ceiling stretch into wide oval windows, revealing the infinite reach of deep space. A giant ringed planet looms beyond, and the rest of the massive station rotates slowly into view, drifting in the void.

Inside, everything feels clean and new. Dark wood flooring adds an unexpected warmth to the sterile luxury.

The menu lists more home options that are locked. He can't afford them, but looking out at the rings of the planet, he doesn't care. Satisfied, he closes it and lets the silence of the stars take over.

INT. SPACE BEDROOM

Bowen slides into the expansive bedroom, where curved windows overlook the alien planet. He looks around, feeling like he's stepped into a dream. It's so much better than what he expected.

>   BOWEN
> Command: record video message.

A floating screen materializes, framing his face, a red dot in the corner.

>   BOWEN
> Mom, I made it. I'm here. Check out this
> place. It's so weird, right? And it feels
> weird. Like... I mean...
>   (bouncing around)
> I knew this technology stimulated the
> brain. But I didn't know it would feel this
> real. It's like I'm really here, you know
> what I mean? Like this is my body and

I'm really moving around. In a real place.
This is impossible. Oh, Oh! You won't
believe this. I see colors! Actual colors,
Mom! I always thought colors would be
a mystery, you know? It's...

He catches himself smiling in the floating screen, happy. Too happy. He clears his throat and straightens his posture, suppressing the excitement.

> BOWEN
> Command: delete message and record a
> new one.

The screen implodes and reappears.

> BOWEN
> Mom, I'm here. I miss you. Don't forget
> to take your meds, okay? And no cheese.
> (smiles)
> Uh, the interview's tomorrow. I'll let you
> know how it goes. Love you. Miss you.
> (pause)
> Command: send to Pastor Lucas.

The screen flashes SENT, then vanishes.

A floating keyboard appears in midair, and as he types, words materialize in magenta.

> Pastor, how's my mom doing? Please

take good care of her. Thank you for everything.

He presses ENTER, and the words fade out.

His worried gaze finds a magic mirror labeled: CUSTOMIZE YOUR BODY.

He slides the age bar to 80, laughing as he watches himself grow older. His hair turns gray, then races back until his head is completely bald and spotted with age. His eyebrows explode into bushy tufts, while his face is ravaged by wrinkles.

He resets his age to 23. An advertisement instantly pops up: "Correct your teeth for ~~$15.99~~ $9.99," displaying a version of Bowen with a perfect smile. His fingers trace the line of his crooked teeth, a row of stubborn misfits refusing to fall in line.

He closes his mouth tight, suddenly ashamed. He never realized how jagged they looked until now. Back home, everyone has a smile like this. Maybe not as crooked as his, but still. With irritation, he waves the message away.

His hair shifts through a spectrum of wild colors – bright pinks, electric blues, glowing greens – before he finally settles on a deep purple. A small smile slips out.

Another ad pops, showing a sexier version of Bowen: "Become your sexiest self. Only ~~$1,299~~ $999." He laughs, half-amused and half-annoyed, then closes it.

Bowen checks the clothing options. He selects a long

black jacket with a big hood, purple parachute pants, and dark orange boots. Not a bad look. And free. Premium clothes hover nearby, but he ignores them. Every dollar counts.

INT. SURVEILLANCE ROOM

A wall of screens monitors people's intimate moments, icons highlighting their emotions, feelings and thoughts. One screen shows Bowen playing with the mirror. Labels flash: EXCITEMENT, GUILT, WORRY. His body leans toward the thrill, but his mind drags him back to fear, for his mother and his soul.

INT. SPACE BEDROOM

Bowen covers a wall with photos of his mother, himself, and their hometown. Hikes. Birthdays. Gardening. Picnics at the lake. Cool robots. Seeing his mother in color for the first time hits hard. Tears rise, but he forces them down with a laugh.

He hangs his favorite photo: an abandoned blue fishing boat covered in snow, sitting in a lonely parking lot in the woods. He stares at it, lips pressed tight together, captivated by a connection he doesn't fully understand.

He forces himself to break the spell and turns, sprawling across a massive, comfy bed, savoring the luxury for the first time, a stark difference from the narrow mattress from back home where he had spent his nights folded in half.

His eyes grow heavy, exhausted from the long trip. As he yawns, he gets a message from the U.W. Port with a courtesy ticket to the Full Moon Festival. It's tonight and it's advertised as the largest music festival in the Worlds.

EXT. FULL MOON FESTIVAL - NIGHT

Bowen comes out of a neon blue arched teleport into an enchanted forest alive with psychedelic lights. Bioluminescent trees stretch overhead, pulsing magenta and blue with the electronic music while giant mushrooms glow through shifting colors. Far ahead, animated projections dance across countless stages.

Wild avatars move and dance everywhere. One has a real third eye. Another is covered in silver feathers – real feathers, not a costume. Everyone is young, cool, beautiful, sexy.

Bowen stumbles upon a VIKING GODDESS with big blue eyes, seemingly in her early 20s, though age here is just a setting. She tosses her golden hair back with a sultry smile, her body swaying to the beat, glowing tattoos pulsing across her skin. He offers a shy smile.

                    VIKING GODDESS
                  (leaning into his ear)
          Cool skins.

She laughs, flashing perfect white teeth, finding Bowen hilariously interesting. In a world of impossible beauty, normal is exotic.

They dance closer, and for a moment, it looks promising. Until Bowen spots the decagon badge on her shoulder. He knows what that yellow symbol with 10 sides means. His excitement dies instantly, and disillusioned, he pushes her away.

> VIKING GODDESS
> Hey! What the fuck?

She shoves Bowen back.

A man resembling the MAD HATTER from *Alice in Wonderland*, with full, thick sideburns and no mustache, watches the scene. He tilts his massive top hat, revealing the words BIOLOGICAL PRIDE stitched across the band.

> MAD HATTER
> (to Bowen, with an English
> accent)
> You good, fam? Is this *upload* botherin'
> ya?

He says "upload" like he means "abomination." Bowen shakes his head, not wanting any trouble, but the Mad Hatter turns on her.

> MAD HATTER
> Stick with your own kind, zombie.

VIKING GODDESS
(scoffs)
Fuck you!
(to Bowen)
And fuck you too.
(looking him up and down)
Here you can be anything and you chose
that?

BOWEN
(to Mad Hatter)
C'mon, it's fine. Leave it alone.

Bowen tries to steer him away, but the Hatter stands firm as a rock.

MAD HATTER
(to Bowen)
Nah, fam. These *zombies* should know better. Humans and uploads don't mix. Me boys would kick her arse.

VIKING GODDESS
Fuck off, you fuckin' purist.

The Mad Hatter eyes her, *be careful*. Bowen steps between them, grabbing the Hatter by the shoulders and forcing him back. People stare.

VIKING GODDESS

You think you're better than me 'cause
I don't have a biological body anymore,
huh? Is that it? You think you can treat
me like this, you piece of shit?

MAD HATTER

Stop actin' like you're bloody human,
yeah? You're not! You're a zombie. No
soul. Just a program. A program imitatin'
who you were before the upload. That's
it. You're disgustin'.

She storms off, flipping them off with both hands. The
hate against uploads is real. They've uploaded their minds, a
process that destroys the brain, killing the body. And they're
discriminated against because of it.

MAD HATTER

I lost me job 'cause of those zombies.
They take shit wages 'cause they don't
have to pay for lifepods or healthcare or
none of that shit like we do. It's a bloody
disgrace, I'm tellin' ya.

Bowen walks away, shaking his head. Too intense. He
just wants to enjoy some good music and take his mind off
his mother for a little while.

On the main stage, a young singer performs in a colorful

cloud-like dress, blending electronic and Latin music.

From the sidelines, Bowen enjoys the music while everyone dances. A group of ancient Egyptians invites him to join, but he pretends not to notice.

The silhouette of a person flying cuts across the dark gold supermoon.

Projections above the stage glitch, freezing, unfreezing, freezing again, then vanishing. The music stops. A gigantic red Möbius strip looms above the stage, rendered in cyberpunk style. It's a twisted, continuous loop with no end, and unlike the infinity symbol, it never crosses itself.

Everyone looks up, awestruck to see people flying. They land on the stage, dressed predominantly in red. They're the famous hacktivist group, Möbius.

LOBA stands at the center, flanked by three members on each side. She is a fearless but haunted hacker in her early 20s, with long dark curls, black wolf ears, and a piercing gaze. Her golden-yellow wolf eyes pop against her darker skin as she scans the audience, filled with rage and sorrow. Thousands of eyes stare back.

Loba takes the singer's microphone and mouths "sorry" to her. She turns to the crowd, her sexy body covered in cool tattoos, the tight golden shorts matching her eyes.

                    LOBA
          Sorry to kill the vibe like this. But this is
          the biggest event in the Worlds.

The musicians exchange confused glances, not knowing what to do. Instead of being annoyed by the interruption, Bowen smiles in surprise.

>   LOBA
>   I know you all love Rhea. She and
>   Franklin created this magical place,
>   where we govern ourselves, right?

Rhea's freckled face materializes as a hologram above the stage, her red-and-white hair blazing. The crowd erupts, chanting Rhea's name, hands raised as if she were a goddess.

>   LOBA
>   Our country is like no other. Yes, we
>   use Tores to vote on laws, and each
>   *biological* citizen gets one Tore. But you
>   need to understand this.

A holographic pie chart materializes above the stage, rendered in cyberpunk style. It shows how voting power is distributed in the United Worlds, with four slices: MYSTERY KEY holds 60% of Tores; RHEA, 20%; RHEA'S SECRET COUNCIL, 10%; THE PEOPLE, 10%.

>   LOBA
>   Our votes don't mean shit!

>   MAD HATTER
>   Fake!

LOBA

Rhea created billions of fake identities
to hoard billions of Tores.

The MYSTERY KEY slice illuminates.

LOBA

That Mystery Key? It belonged to Rhea
and Franklin. It holds almost 4. Billion.
Tores. And you know what? Something
happened to it 'cause it hasn't been used
in the last 18 years. Not since the night
Rhea killed Franklin.

The crowd gasps and murmurs.

LOBA

Yeah, her own husband... That's who
Rhea truly is.
(waves the Mystery Key away)
Even without those Tores...

The MYSTERY KEY slice vanishes. The remaining slices
expand, showing Rhea controls half of what's left.

LOBA

Rhea, and 12 industry titans who report
to her, still control the majority. *They*
decide. They always have.

MAD HATTER

What do you care? Uploads can't vote!

The Hatter laughs at his own insult.

LOBA

Rhea sends us to prison and tortures us for no reason. No reason other than for speaking an inconvenient truth she doesn't want you to hear.

The projections shift to footage of people on fire. They shake in agony, chained to stone walls in dark dungeons, burning but never dying.

LOBA

This should make you furious! You feel the agony of burning alive, but never die.

MAD HATTER

Fake! Jog on, you fuckin' *zombie*!

LOBA

Rhea's a fucking dictator! She rules like a God. Keeps watch on everyone. She knows when you wake up. What you do. Who you hang out with. What you talk about. What makes you happy, sad, afraid. Who you love. Hate. She knows it all.

(scoffs)

She even knows what you dream, for fuck's sake. And your memories? Your most private moments? She knows all of them.

UNITED WORLDS SOLDIERS come out from the distant neon portals of the entrance. Led by GENERAL ZEFFROSS, they fly toward the main stage in dark blue camouflage uniforms and high-tech helmets with reflective blue visors that hide their eyes.

Loba signals her crew, who take flight, tossing cool Möbius necklaces into the crowd.

LOBA

She knows everyone's fucking secrets. There's no place to hide.

(holding up a Möbius necklace)

Except when you wear one of these. This blocks the trackers. Use them. Protect yourselves!

J.S. remains by her side. He is tall and athletic, his face painted in tribal war style. Four muscular arms complete his intimidating frame.

J.S.

(pulls Loba's arm)

Loba! C'mon. Let's go!

LOBA
(engrossed in the people)
Together we must reclaim the power to
govern ourselves. A power that belongs
to all of us, biological *and* artificial. We
must demand the right to privacy and
the freedom to speak without fear.
(pause)
We're just exposing their lies. And
encouraging you... to open your eyes!

J.S. pulls Loba away, and they launch into the air, tossing
necklaces to the crowd. Bowen grabs one from Loba, staring
at her, starstruck.

General Zeffross fires. He misses Loba but hits three
spectators, who collapse instantly, eyes open, motionless.

The General keeps chasing Loba through the air. Bullets
fly close as she zigzags, throwing necklaces. One shot almost
hits her hand. She turns translucent, like a ghost, and flies
straight toward the entrance. Bullets pass through her like air,
though she can no longer hold the necklaces.

As Loba approaches the neon blue arch, she turns solid
again and disappears through the portal.

Frustrated, Zeffross switches the selector mode on his
rifle from PARALYZE to KILL, turning his black weapon
golden. He tracks the flight of a MÖBIUS MEMBER... and
fires.

The bullet tears through the air and slams into the man's stomach.

INT. CLANDESTINE PORT - CONTINUOUS

Inside his brain, glowing pulses flash in chaos between neurons like an electric storm.

His biological body suffers extremely painful seizures inside a lifepod.

An alarm beeps. The health monitor flashes with a message: NEUROTOXICITY ALERT: ELEVATED GLUTAMATE LEVELS.

He shakes violently... until he finally goes still. The monitor updates: "USER STATUS: BRAIN ACTIVITY CEASED."

EXT. FULL MOON FESTIVAL - CONTINUOUS

The Möbius member drops from the sky, crashing onto the cap of a giant glowing mushroom. He slides off the rubbery surface and thuds into the grass, lying dead as the mushroom pulses rhythmically above him.

Panic sweeps the crowd. Everyone rushes toward the neon portals, tossing the necklaces Möbius gave out. No one trusts hackers.

BOWEN
(to himself)
Command: show me the chart Möbius

just shared. With the Tores.

A glowing message appears in midair, read aloud by a friendly voice. "Sorry, Bowen. I can't reproduce false information. Do you wish to report suspicious activity?"

> BOWEN
> (rolls his green eyes)
> So what about those missing Tores? The ones in the Mystery Key. There's gotta be evidence they exist, right?

A beautiful, sharp-looking ASSISTANT materializes, glowing to signal she's a hologram. Only her upper body is visible.

> ASSISTANT
> (friendly voice)
> That's a common piece of misinformation spread by the criminal group Möbius. But the truth is very simple. Those Tores aren't missing. They belong to citizens who don't vote or who are dead. You know, each citizen has one Tore, but participation isn't mandatory. Voting is a right, not an obligation.
> (pause)
> Would you like me to explain how laws are proposed or how votes are cast?

Bowen waves his hand, making her vanish instantly. He admires the necklace: a Möbius-shaped silver ring.

MAD HATTER
(pointing to Bowen's necklace)
You better chuck it, fam. Don't fall for
their bullshit. Those freaks will hack you
with it.

Bowen puts the necklace on with a defiant look.

QUICK SHOT of a wall of screens monitoring people.
The feed showing Bowen at the festival goes dead, replaced
by a message: TRACKING ERROR.

MAD HATTER
Fam, I'm tryna help. And if soldiers see
ya with that...

Bowen turns away, slipping the necklace under his shirt.
As a security engineer, he knows Möbius, but the idea that
the world might not be what it seems strikes a deep chord
in him.

Chapter 3
She isn't real

19 min read

Previously...

Bowen rented a lifepod capsule to enter the United Worlds. He was shocked by how real everything felt. For the first time in his life, he saw colors.

At a music festival, he danced with a Viking goddess but recoiled when he noticed the decagon badge on her shoulder, marking her as an upload. Uploads are people who permanently transfer their minds into the United Worlds, destroying their biological bodies in the process.

The festival was interrupted by Möbius, a famous hacktivist group led by Loba. She claimed Rhea, the creator of the United Worlds, secretly holds the majority of Tores and spies on everyone. She warned that the only protection is a Möbius necklace that blocks trackers. Bowen took one and put it on.

INT. ABI'S BEDROOM - MORNING

Sunlight filters through the moth-eaten holes in the multi-colored curtains, illuminating dust particles drifting in the air.

Bowen's mother, Abi, winces as she tries to sit up in bed, clutching her side, catching her breath. She swallows two pills with a sip of water, then stares at nothing, her eyes puffy from crying.

A knock at the door makes her jump.

OLD MAN'S VOICE

Abi, sweetheart. May I come in?

She straightens her back, buttons her wool sweater, and

smooths her gray hair back with her skeletal hands.

ABI

Come in, Pastor.

PASTOR LUCAS pokes his head in. He's 65, with a long black-gray beard and a ponytail, wearing tiny round glasses and a cracked leather headband.

LUCAS

How are you feeling? Sleep well?

She gives a tight-lipped smile and nods, her eyes insisting she's better than she is.

LUCAS

From your son.
(gives her a small device)
And you can record a message for him.
If you'd like.

She closes her eyes and bows, a silent *thank you.*

LUCAS

I'll take out the trash, okay? Take your time.

ABI

Pastor, wait. May I ask you a favor? Don't say anything to anyone, please. I don't want people knowing where my son is.

He nods and closes the door, the only one who knows of his son's sin.

She waits a few seconds for Pastor Lucas to get out of earshot, and as his footsteps fade, she plays Bowen's message. Knowing he is risking his soul in that sinful place just to save her... it breaks her. She is unable to hold back her tears.

INT. CHURCH - MORNING

Pastor Lucas preaches to a packed congregation. Sunlight streams through stained glass, painting the floor in a mosaic of colors.

Abi's eyes fall to the empty space beside her, the absence louder than the sermon.

INT. BOWEN'S SPACE BEDROOM

Bowen lies in bed, surrounded by screens, practicing for his interview. He does coding exercises, electronic music pulsing from every angle.

His eyes drift to the alien planet outside the curved windows. He stares without seeing, lost in thought.

An incoming message snaps him back.

He opens a video from his mother. She sits in her dark bedroom, her face half-hidden in the shadows, likely on purpose.

ABI (ON VIDEO)

Bowie...

(pause)

I'm doing very well. The pain hasn't been too bad. I'm taking my meds. And I'm not eating cheese. Not even a little. You'd be proud.

(smiles)

The neighbors bring me food and check on me. Pastor Lucas is a saint. Visits twice a day.

(pause)

Okay, son, don't wanna bother you. Good luck with your interview. You'll do great. You're so smart. I'm sorry my health forced you to go to that...

(voice breaking)

Godless place. Be careful. Be careful with the illusions of that satanic world. And don't get into trouble. Please.

(pause)

I miss you. I love you so so much, Bo-Bo. You...

Abi tries to say goodbye, but words don't come out. She just waves, and the message ends.

Bowen stares down, scratching his neck, anxious. He

needs this job. He needs the money. He needs to save her. And he needs to save her before it's too late.

Taking a deep breath, he forces himself back to coding.

* * *

Bowen tosses and turns in his bed, unable to fall asleep. The heavy silence keeps his mind racing.

A notification materializes.

> Need help sleeping? We'll have you out
> in 30 seconds.

Bowen frowns, annoyed by the creepy precision, and waves it away.

> BOWEN
> Command: show me a summary of news
> about the United Worlds. Anything
> relevant to a security engineer interview.

A floating screen appears.

> ANCHOR (ON VIDEO)
> Crime is at a record low. Since United
> Worlds citizens passed the death penalty
> for hackers, crime has dropped 40%.
> The zero-tolerance stance on hacking is
> one of the most important policies since
> the U.W. was founded. Officials say these
> measures are keeping the Worlds safe

and –

He swipes to the next report.

> ANCHOR (ON VIDEO)
> Human unemployment hits 22% as inflation soars. Companies are replacing humans with uploads to cut costs.

> BOWEN
> Command: Yes, okay, help me sleep. And wake me up in 4 hours.

"Inducing sleep now..." His eyelids grow heavy. An ad plays with Rhea promoting Secret Vaults.

> RHEA (ON VIDEO)
> Passwords can be cracked. Faces can be faked. But thieves can't fake your mind. That's why I trust Secret Vaults. It scans your brain –

As he falls asleep, the screen vanishes.

* * *

Bowen sleeps curled on the edge of the massive bed, as if he were still sleeping on the narrow mattress back home. So much empty space around him, untouched, sheets still neatly tucked.

An alarm goes off. With a snap of his fingers, he silences

it instantly.

INT. DEEP FANTASY CABARET - NIGHT

A big pink neon sign reads, *Deep Fantasy* and a smaller one below, *Fuck your favorite movie stars.*

Vibrant pink light washes over everything in the immense cabaret, where bodies move on dance platforms surrounded by shouting crowds. Smoke and laughter rise toward the high ceiling, its surface covered with spotlights.

Da Vinci's MONA LISA in person, looking extremely hot, welcomes guests at the entrance.

MONA LISA
(smiling to Bowen)
Welcome to Deep Fantasy. We offer the wildest fantasies. Experiences beyond your imagination. How can I help you, sweetie?

Bowen smooths his messy purple hair and clears his dry throat.

BOWEN
Uh, I have a job interview. For the Security Engineer position?

She points to the second floor where two men are arguing.

As he heads for the stairs, he weaves through a gallery of living fantasies. On one side, sexy models show off their bodies under pink spotlights, pink price tags glowing above their heads. On the other, DeepFakes of famous actors and actresses perform scenes from iconic movies.

And it gets wilder with each step he takes. A man with broad shoulders, his muscles shaped like hard labor made them, wears tight shorts that reveal two big cocks. A woman with an hourglass figure and three voluptuous breasts turns, revealing two more on her back. Over her shoulder, she catches Bowen's eye and winks. As she spins back around, her hands slide under his shirt, fingers tracing his chest. He shakes her off, and in that motion, his Möbius necklace slips into view, too freaked out to notice.

Upstairs, the two guys continue arguing. One is the SECURITY MANAGER, a neurotic man in his 30s with restless eyes, his irises pink like a rabbit's. The other is DON LEE, late 20s, easygoing and handsome, with a glowing yellow tattoo splitting his lower lip.

SECURITY MANAGER

But the position has been filled!

BOWEN

...I'm here for the interview?

The manager storms past them. Don laughs, adjusting his round yellow-tinted sunglasses, the lenses catching the club's pink lights.

BOWEN

You think this is funny?

DON

(whiskey voice)

No, sorry man. I didn't mean to. I came
for the interview too. Sorry.

(notices Bowen's necklace)

Hey, lemme buy you a drink.

Bowen hesitates. He doesn't trust this guy. But two
minutes ago, he still had hope of saving his mother. Now,
in a matter of seconds, that plan is shattered, leaving him
completely lost. He needs a drink. Or two.

Back downstairs, Bowen and Don drink beers at a table
near a dance platform. Exotic dancers seduce guests as they
move to a sexy, apocalyptic blues-rock anthem. Don fixes
his short locs, tying them tighter into a messy topknot. His
bright orange T-shirt catches Bowen's eye, the text bold and
defiant: WE ARE ALL HUMAN.

Bowen lifts the beer to his nose and frowns, not believing
how real it smells. He takes a sip and smiles in surprise. It
even tastes like the real thing.

DON

Man, before the recession, I could
choose where to work. But now?

Don notices Bowen is distracted by the sexy dancers.

                    DON

I know. Best sex I ever had, man. Porn's
a joke next to this, am I right?

                    BOWEN

What? No. That's too weird. Fucking
uploads would be like fucking a different
species.
          (checks Don's shoulder)
Fuck. You're not an upload, right?

Don laughs, showing his bare shoulder. Bowen eyes the
dancers, each with a yellow decagon badge on theirs.

                    DON

You know, they're not uploads. They
have to wear those badges like uploads
do, which by the way, is dehumanizing
for uploads, but they're DeepFakes.

                    BOWEN

C'mon. Uploads, DeepFakes... same shit.

                    DON

What? No, man. DeepFakes are like this
table, or your clothes. It has no feelings
or thoughts. No consciousness. It's an
empty shell that looks like a person, and
it's programmed to follow commands.

But it's a shell. A beautiful, sexy, wild shell.

(chuckles)

But uploads? Yeah, man. They're like you and me. They're people who uploaded their consciousness and don't have a biological body anymore. You know, uploading destroys the bio brain, killing the bio body, but it creates an artificial brain that's exactly the same. And it's stimulated by an artificial body. Like yours is right now.

Bowen gives him a side-eye.

A message flashes in midair, visible only to Bowen.

LOW FUNDS: Renew your plan to stay in the United Worlds.

A reminder of the reality awaiting him back home. He chugs his beer.

DON

So anyway, how long have you been a Security Engineer?

BOWEN

I'm not. I mean... I don't have certifications and all that. But I know how to do it. I taught myself.

Don nods, impressed.

> BOWEN
>
> I think they invited me to interview only 'cause they were recruiting people in Tahoe. You know, to be close to their data center.

> DON
>
> Yeah, I'm on the Nevada side. You?

> BOWEN
>
> San Francisco right now. Got a coupon for a port here. But I'm from Homewood.

> DON
>
> Fuck off! Homewood? For real? I'm from Homewood! Who are you?

They stare at each other, shocked to meet someone from their hometown in the United Worlds, especially in a virtual cabaret.

> BOWEN
>
> ...I'm Bowen Huxley.

> DON
>
> Huxley? No way. You're Abi's kid?
> (chuckles)

Oh, God. She hated me. Well, who didn't, right? What are you doing here?

Don taps a button on the table, materializing an unlabeled bottle of electric blue liquor. He pours two shots and hands one to Bowen. *Clink.* They slam it. Bowen coughs, wincing. Strong stuff. He tries to wash it down with beer, and coughs again.

> BOWEN
>
> ...And you are?

> DON
>
> Donna Lee?

> BOWEN
>
> Donna? Yeh, I remember her. She never took shit from no one. And people gave her a lotta shit.
>
> (coughs)
>
> What? Is she your sister? I don't remember her having a brother.

Don lights a cigarette, flashing a naughty smile as he waits for Bowen to realize.

> BOWEN
>
> ...You're Donna?

                    DON

I'm Don now. I'm finally me, what can I
say? How've you been, man?

Don offers him a smoke. Bowen waves it away but grabs
the bottle, pouring two more shots. *Clink.*

                  BOWEN
        (coughing, looking at the drink)
Jesus. Fuck.
        (clears throat)
Not gonna lie, the day you beat up Izak?
You kinda became a legend for me. You
left after that, right?

                    DON

Couldn't stay a minute longer, man. I'm
lucky I was able to get outta Homewood
alive. Fucking hated it.

                  BOWEN

I'm heading back there.

                    DON

What? Fuck that. No you're not.

                  BOWEN

Yeh. My mom's not doing well. She
needs a kidney. She doesn't have too

much time. But you don't know how fucking expensive it is. That's why I'm here, actually. The job was gonna pay me enough to cover it. You know, to cover it before it's too late.

Don looks away, thinking.

> BOWEN
>
> Look, no offense, Don, but this fake world's a joke. Sure, it has... its things. I'll give you that. Things happened here I didn't think were possible. But c'mon. You know that none of this is real. This is just an illusion. People come here to avoid reality. You shouldn't waste your life in here. The real world's out there. Artificial life isn't real life. It's not natural.

Don narrows his eyes, blowing smoke in a slow... steady stream, tinted pink by the club's lights.

> DON
>
> You hungry?

> BOWEN
>
> Fucking starving. I could even eat chicken. And I eat that every day back home. Is something wrong with my pod?

                    DON

They make you feel all body sensations.
Even uploads that don't have bio bodies.
          (leans closer)
And I have this theory: when you don't
spend much, they make you hungrier.
          (pouring two more shots)
C'mon, I know this place where you can
eat polar bears and weird shit.

Bowen stares at him, incredulous.

                    DON

Well, you don't really eat it. You know,
the pod just tells your brain what it tastes
like.
          (smokes)
C'mon, man, don't you wanna taste
something you can't find anywhere else?

Don slams the shot and drains the beer. He stands up,
jerking his head toward the exit. Bowen leans back, thinking
about it.

Fuck it. This might be his last night in the United Worlds.
He downs the alcohol and his anxiety.

EXT. SAFARI RESTAURANT - NIGHT

An open-air restaurant sits deep in the tropical rainforest, exposed to the starry sky. Dim red lights cast a warm glow over the tables.

Bowen and Don lean in, laughing hard, super drunk. Between them, the electric blue liquor bottle is nearly empty.

> BOWEN
>
> So I built a robot in the 6th grade, right? And-and... Pastor Lucas... He-he... he held an exorcism!
>
> (both laugh)
>
> For me and the robot!

They roar with laughter, the sound so contagious that people at nearby tables join in.

> BOWEN
>
> (mimicking throwing holy water)
>
> "Vade retro Satana! Vade retro Satana!"

They crack up again. Don laughs so hard, he topples off his chair. People stare, amused. Bowen tries to control himself, shushing Don as he helps him up.

> BOWEN
>
> (wiping tears away, rubbing his sore jaw)
>
> God, my face hurts. Can't remember the last time I laughed this hard.
>
> (deep breath, tone shifts)
>
> Which is fucked up. Nothing's real here.

Don chuckles under his breath, lifting his eyebrows, his eyes saying, *yeah, right.*

Their burgers materialize. Bowen takes a bite, closing his eyes to savor the juicy flavor.

> BOWEN
>
> Mmm. What the fuck? Is this really what
> polar bears taste like? Jesus.
> (laughs)
> This is the best I've ever had. Want
> some?

A commotion erupts near the entrance.

> RESTAURANT MANAGER
>
> I said get up! You can't sit here!

Don turns his head. The restaurant manager is looming over a young couple, pointing aggressively at the door. The pair wears decagon badges on their shoulders. They stand up, heads bowed in humiliation, trying to disappear as diners stare.

As the manager shoves them toward the exit, Don stands up and blocks their path.

> DON
>
> (to the manager)
> Hey. What's the problem?

RESTAURANT MANAGER

Sir, please step aside. They were just leaving.

DON

You're kicking them out. Is that it?

RESTAURANT MANAGER

It's our policy. We don't serve uploads.

DON

You don't wanna be like that, man. C'mon. Let them eat.

The manager shakes his head with an indifferent shrug and tries to push past.

DON

If they leave, we leave.

RESTAURANT MANAGER

I'm sorry you feel that way, sir.

The manager side-steps Don, forcing the couple out the door. Don turns to Bowen, waiting for backup, but Bowen is busy devouring his burger.

DON

(to Bowen)

C'mon. Let's get outta here.

BOWEN

Nah, I'm good.

(takes a big bite)

Mmm. So fuckin' good.

Don scratches his ear, stung by the lack of support. He looks away, then throws himself back into his chair, draining the last drops from the bottle.

DON

So tell me. How did you learn security engineering without a pod?

BOWEN

Oh, I built a VR headset. Using old parts.

Don raises his eyebrows in astonishment.

BOWEN

Took me forever to find all the parts, you know? But I love it. It can't send signals to the brain, so, you know, no full immersion. But it reads brain signals. It's magical. I can move my avatar using just my thoughts.

Bowen's face lights up with wonder.

Don, impressed again, taps the table, and a polarized capsule forms around them, sealing them in complete privacy. He pulls out a Möbius necklace from beneath his shirt.

DON
(showing his necklace)
I saw you have one too, right?

BOWEN
I got this one from Loba.

DON
What? No way. Really? Oh man, the best hacker in the world. Total. Badass. Fucking legend. And so fucking hot, am I right?

BOWEN
(grimacing)
But it's an upload, right?

DON
She is an upload. Yes. Who fuckin' cares, man?

BOWEN
...It doesn't exist in the real world. It... okay. *She* isn't real.

DON
Don't be a purist, man. And stop saying this place isn't real, 'kay? Outside, everything is made of atoms. Here?

Everything is made of qubits. Quantum bytes. So fuckin' what, man? That doesn't make either one less real.

(leaning in)

Do you really care so much about what things are made of? This isn't an "illusion." What happens here happens. The United Worlds is as real as Homewood, man. Don't be so closed-minded like everyone back home. You're clearly smarter than that.

(before Bowen responds)

Anyway, hear me out...

Don takes a few quick bites of his burger, wipes his hands, and spreads an animated poster on the table: HACKER TOURNAMENT.

DON

It's two per team. I could use your help.

BOWEN

(laughing, pointing to the poster)

With what? This?

Don nods, his eyebrows arched in a knowing smile. Bowen laughs so hard, he nearly tips his chair over. Don takes off his sunglasses and leans forward.

DON

C'mon, man. I'm serious. You know about security. Many great hackers started that way.

BOWEN

Oh, I'm not laughing about that. I know how to
        (lowering his voice)
hack, okay? It's fun. But they kill hackers here. You crazy? This talk can get us killed.

DON

But it's safe. They organize it every year. Bowen, c'mon. $250k first prize. And that's U.W. dollars, not American. I mean...
        (pause)
How much do you need for your mom?

As Don pours two more shots, Bowen leans back, intoxicated. He bites his nails, studying the proposal. It's an impossible bet, a dangerous one. But the prize is enough to save his mother's life.

Chapter 4
Die in a place that isn't real

26 min read

Previously...

Bowen didn't get the job but met Don, a man he knew from back home. They spent the night drinking and bonding.

Impressed by Bowen's self-taught engineering skills and needing a partner, Don invited him to an illegal hacker tournament. The penalty is execution, but the prize is enough to save Bowen's mother.

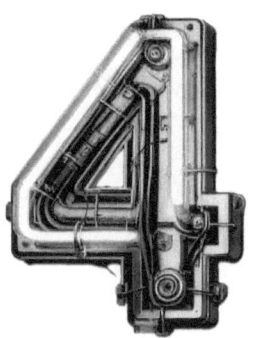

INT. BOWEN'S HOUSE - MORNING

The weathered door creaks open, sunlight slipping into the dark cabin.

BOWEN

Mom, I'm home!

The room feels wrong. The camping string lights, which should be outside, drape across the ceiling beams, buzzing faintly with a flickering beat. Dirty dishes pile high in the sink and on the kitchen counter. Clothes, books, and boxes litter the floor, while pills and used pen-injectors scatter across the coffee table. Above the fireless fireplace, black block letters spell HELP.

His mother isn't there.

Worried, he rushes to her room. He freezes in the doorway. A motionless shape lies under the covers, completely hidden.

> BOWEN

Mom?

The shape doesn't move. He walks to the bed, floorboards creaking, and peels the covers back...

Black ants swarm his mother's dead body, devouring her.

INT. BOWEN'S SPACE BEDROOM

Bowen wakes up, agitated, gasping for air.

A magenta message hovers in the dark.

> Would you like to delete the nightmare?

He ignores it, checking for messages from Pastor Lucas on a floating screen. Nothing. He exhales, relieved. No news is good news. But the weight returns just as fast. He scratches his head, thinking of the hacker tournament. It has to work. It has to.

It needs to.

INT. MAZE - NIGHT

A massive square maze spans the area of four football fields. Its concrete walls shift in color as they wind inward: yellow at the outer edge, orange in the middle, and red at the center, where the only exit awaits. 30 teams stand ready at their assigned starting points along the perimeter.

High above in the stands, a COMMENTATOR appears as a hologram, surrounded by a cheerful holographic crowd. The stands are just projections, as everyone watches safely from home. Only the competitors are really here, for security reasons.

> COMMENTATOR
>
> If you're just joining up to the best hacker tournament in the Worlds, listen up. Since the death penalty passed, fewer and fewer teams compete each year. Only the best, the brave or the desperate dare to show up. But viewership? Breaking records! You all love the danger, don't you?
>
> (smiles)
>
> Players must hack their way through the maze, capturing flags for points. First team out of the maze wins. But catch this: if the maze detects they're hackers, they lose all points and are disqualified.

Bowen and Don stand by their assigned entrance, tense, rocking from side to side, waiting for the tournament to start. A name tag reading WOODBYTE floats over them, identifying their team. They're ready to hack, their hands on the keyboards, eyes on the big screens.

Bowen gets another message from the U.W. Port, flashing in midair, visible only to him.

> LAST WARNING:
> EXIT IMMEDIATELY.
> You've exceeded your paid access time
> in the United Worlds. Insufficient funds
> to continue.

A memory flashes FROM BOWEN'S POV (B&W): Bowen's mother scratches herself too much as she puts together a puzzle on the coffee table with her skeletal hands. She has dark circles around her swollen eyes.

The memory ends.

Bowen thinks of her. He thinks how desperately she needs the treatment, how little time she has left. This might be the last chance to save her.

He snaps out of it at the blare of a trumpet, the crowd exploding around him. Above the maze, a giant sandglass timer floats in the air, its grains draining from one chamber to the other.

> DON
> Command: discover IP addresses and
> open ports.

> BOWEN
> Command: check for OS fingerprinting.

COMMENTATOR

They're studying the maze tech, looking
for flaws in the system, vulnerabilities to
exploit.

Their screens flash with NOT FOUND and FORBIDDEN
messages while other teams capture flags and celebrate.

Don finally gets a breakthrough and opens one of the
files, listing software versions.

DON

Druver! I've hacked Druver before.
Command: search exploits for Druver
v7.

As Don types and hits ENTER, a success message appears:
"Administrator user created!" A yellow keycard materializes.
He grabs it to open the door.

They race through the maze, its yellow concrete walls
chipped and peeling. Around the corner, they find a yellow
flag and clasp hands.

BOWEN

(turning the flag)
Look! A hint. "Silence your mind to find
the ultimate answer."

The scoreboard shows they're still near the bottom, in
one of the last positions.

A low vibration crawls up the walls, barely noticeable at

first. Then, an earthquake rattles the maze, sending tremors through its intricate paths. The yellow outer edge cracks and collapses, chunks of the ground plunging into a black abyss.

> COMMENTATOR
>
> Oh yes! My favorite part. Players who fall into the void keep their points but are eliminated.

Players scramble as the destruction creeps inward, some slipping into the void. The center holds, for now...

Don and Bowen sprint through a long corridor, its yellow walls fading into orange.

Don swipes his keycard at a metallic door, but the panel flashes ACCESS DENIED. This door has a keypad.

Don pounds his keyboard. Bowen types slower, with precision. Type. Enter. UNAUTHORIZED. Type. Enter. FORBIDDEN. The ground falls into the void 30 feet behind them. 29 feet. 28.

The speakers above the door blast an electronic track, its pulsating bassline growing louder and louder.

> DON
> (shouting upward)
> You think you could turn it up a little more? I can still hear myself think, you know?

BOWEN

"Silence your mind to find the ultimate
answer."

Bowen opens the audio file of the song playing in the maze, then loads the original track. He overlays the two sound waves, noticing a mismatch. The waveforms don't align. Subtle changes in the amplitude reveal a pattern, a hidden code.

Bowen extracts bits from those differences.

Behind them, the void keeps creeping in, inching closer. They're trapped. There's no going back. Bits transform into characters. One. By. One.

BOWEN

C'mon, c'mon, c'mon.

The last character reveals itself. Bowen punches the password into the keypad, each key producing a unique tone. The screen flashes ACCESS DENIED, red lights blinking. He tries again, the keys chiming like musical notes, but the result is the same: ACCESS DENIED.

The door remains locked. *What the hell?*

The void is 4 feet away. Elimination is seconds away.

Bowen nods, his head bobbing to the song's heavy rhythm. *Aha, that's it!*

The void is 1 foot away.

Bowen presses the keys again, this time mimicking the

song's rhythm, matching the beat blasting from the speakers.

The metallic door swirls into a portal. The ground gives way beneath their heels... but they jump through the portal just in time. They land hard in a new section of the maze, closer to the center.

Sprawled on the floor, they spot a red flag imprinted with a blueprint of the maze.

The scoreboard updates and WOODBYTE rockets to second place.

In the stands, a mysterious, stylish young woman smiles and applauds. She looks like a Hindu goddess, with hazel eyes and large silver earrings dangling down to her shoulders.

> COMMENTATOR
>
> We've seen history today, folks! First time a rookie team solves the hardest challenge of all.

Guided by the blueprint, Bowen and Don navigate through the maze with ease, skipping challenges and slipping through the correct portals. The paint-peeled orange walls deepen into red, and as they round the corner, they spot a red door with a glowing EXIT sign.

> DON
>
> Oh man! This is it.

On other parts of the maze, competitors fall into the dark abyss. The maze is disintegrating. Only the red center holds.

Bowen and Don are laser-focused, hacking the last door. If they crack it, they'll become the champions. Bowen codes much faster than before, carried away by the adrenaline. He knows what he is doing. Probably.

> DON
> Hey. Bo. Easy. Take your time. Look at
> the board.

Bowen ignores him, typing furiously. Aside from being a tech genius, he is stubborn as hell.

> DON
> Hey. Bowen. Be careful, okay? We have
> the points to make a lotta money. But
> if we get caught, we walk away with
> nothing. Bowen? You hear –?

A cage materializes around them, trapping them. A red message flashes in front of them.

> SYSTEM ALERT: HACKING
> DETECTED

The scoreboard drops WOODBYTE from second place to last. Zero points.

> BOWEN
> No! Fuck! Fuck, fuck, fuck, fuck. Fuck!

Bowen rattles the cage bars, screaming. Don just shakes his head, lifting his eyebrows, his eyes saying, *told ya.*

* * *

A floating platform hovers above the maze, the yellow and orange sections restored as if they never crumbled. Competitors sit facing the stage, where the commentator stands next to a row of trophies and medals. He is no longer a hologram, as he needs to be solid to hand out the awards.

The tournament has ended, and with it, Bowen's hope of saving his mother. He buries his face in his hands. Don rubs his back to comfort him, knowing how hard this defeat hits his new friend.

COMMENTATOR

Before we introduce the winners, the award for Best Player, and a $50k prize, goes to... Bones! From team WoodByte!

The holographic crowd erupts. Don nudges Bowen, who sits frozen, not realizing.

DON

Go! He said, "Bones." You won!

Don hauls Bowen, who stands slowly with disbelief. He stumbles onto the stage and accepts the MVP medal, unsure they got it right. He smiles, raising his hands with his palms up, having no idea what's going on.

Back on his seat, Bowen shows Don the medal. In the polished gold, a reflection shifts...

SOLDIERS dive from the sky.

Dozens of them fly in dark blue camouflage uniforms and high-end helmets. They open fire, slaughtering everyone. Even those who surrender are killed.

Don kicks his chair onto its side and scrambles behind it. Bowen could hide too. He should. But he doesn't. He just sits there, frozen, bullets flying past. Don grabs his jacket and drags him down to cover.

Everyone runs in panic. Bullets strike hackers, who collapse, violently twitching in deadly seizures.

In the physical world, their bodies thrash against the walls of their lifepods, dying alone in the dark.

BOWEN

There's gotta be an emergency command
to exit the Worlds, right?

DON

What? No! Run!

Chaos. Total. Chaos. People scramble for their lives, dodging streams of bullets. They leap off the platform, dropping back into the maze to hunt for exit portals.

Don, Bowen, and five more hackers sprint down a long hallway with an exit portal glowing at the end. Behind them, General Zeffross advances, killing effortlessly. They jump over those who are shaking on the ground, dying.

Don escapes through the portal. 20 feet back, Bowen trips

over someone who's just been shot by Zeffross. He scrambles up and runs for his life. The portal is 15 feet away... 10... 5...

The portal slams shut. No escape now. The only way out is back the way he came... through Zeffross.

Bowen stands alone... and accepts his brief life.

A blue laser dot burns his forehead. He shuts his eyes, wincing, bracing for impact.

A memory flashes FROM BOWEN'S POV (B&W): Bowen hugs his mother outside the cabin, bathed in morning light, the day he left for the United Worlds.

The memory ends.

Zeffross shoots Bowen in the head.

CUT TO BLACK.

Everything goes black.

In the sudden darkness, there is complete silence.

No screams.

No breath.

No heartbeat.

Nothing.

Then, a sharp, high-pitched ringing begins. It rises steadily, growing louder and louder to a deafening, piercing shriek that refuses to end.

INT. ROOM #2222 - CONTINUOUS

Bowen gasps, clawing at his chest as he hyperventilates. The saleswoman stares, her wide eyes saying, *what the fuck?*

> SALESWOMAN
> ...Are you okay?

Bowen is having a panic attack. He stumbles out of the lifepod, disoriented, and crashes to his knees, a soul clawing its way back from the dead. With his hands on the floor, he breathes heavily, taking gulps of air as if he had been drowning. His wild eyes scan the minimalist room, bathed in futuristic ambient light, purple and blue.

> SALESWOMAN
> Sorry. I had to disconnect you. We sent
> you a bunch of messages. If you want to
> stay longer, you need to pay.

She doesn't know she just saved his life. The lifepod was seconds away from frying his brain.

INT. MAZE - CONTINUOUS

General Zeffross is intrigued by Bowen's avatar. No seizures, unlike the others. He sticks a round device between Bowen's eyebrows and circles his fingers over it clockwise, activating it. A message materializes.

> Tracing...

After two seconds, it flashes: UNTRACEABLE.

He looks inside Bowen's shirt and rips his Möbius necklace off and tries again.

Tracing...

EXT. UNITED WORLDS PORT - MORNING

Bowen bursts out of the stylish building, which is wrapped in colorful W-shaped tiles, and runs down the street.

He sprints down the dirty stairs into the subway.

On the platform, he hugs his duffel bag to his chest, biting his nails. His eyes dart across the empty station, expecting soldiers in every shadow.

Headlights sweep the dark tunnel as the train screeches in.

He steps into the subway car.

The subway emerges from the tunnel, sunlight washing over Bowen's face as it becomes an overland train.

At a train station, he hides behind a column, then hops onto the next train, using his duffel bag as cover. He sits facing the floor-to-ceiling windows.

Countryside gives way to mountains and winding rivers.

At dusk, the train snakes along a steep slope, lost among mountains thick with autumn forests. The sky burns orange and rose-pink.

Night finds him fighting sleep in a cold bus station.

By dawn, a self-driving bus glides down the highway. Inside, orange marker lights glow faintly in the dark cabin. Bowen sits alone in the back, headphones on. He wears his AR safety goggles from the power plant to talk to Don, who appears as a hologram.

> DON (AS A HOLOGRAM)
> Man, I'm sorry. I really am. Look, there's an empty pod where I am. I'll save it for you, okay?

> BOWEN
> Don't. I'm not going back. My mom needs me here. You know, where things matter?
> (scoffs)
> Can't believe we almost died in a place that isn't even real.

INT./EXT. HOMEWOOD MAIN STREET - BUS - DUSK

The bus winds along the lake, the water reflecting the autumn trees.

Bowen sleeps with his beanie pulled over half his face, slumped against the window.

The last part of the conversation they were having plays back.

> DON (VOICE OVER)
> Die in a place that isn't real? C'mon, Bo...
> You don't really think this place is fake,
> do you? Like you said, we almost died.
> How can you die if this isn't real?

The bus halts, jolting Bowen awake. He pulls his beanie up and checks outside, worried he missed his stop. He hasn't.

His green eyes pop against his pale face, dazed from the stress of almost dying and lack of rest. Too many hours traveling. Squinting, he sees thick black smoke rising from the mountains, far away.

EXT. DIRT MOUNTAIN ROAD - DUSK

Smoke billows above the canopy. Red emergency lights strobe through the towering pines swaying in the wind.

Bowen races up a narrow dirt road that spirals through the forest, heart pounding. The deep thrum of an engine grows louder. And louder.

He rounds the last bend.

His house is engulfed in flames.

Neighbors and firefighters scramble to extinguish the fire, but it's too late. Total destruction is certain. The battle now is to stop the spread, to keep the flames from claiming the rest.

Bowen runs toward the flames, but a FIREFIGHTER catches him, holding him back with a firm grip.

FIREFIGHTER

Bowen! She's not in there! Your mother
is not in there.

BOWEN

(breathes again, uneven)

So where is she, Frank? Mom! Mom!

The firefighter squeezes Bowen's shoulder and looks
away, unable to meet his eyes.

BOWEN

Hey! Who knows where she is? Frank,
c'mon. Where is she?

Frank stays silent. Bowen staggers back, stepping on
something soft. It's one of his mother's slippers. He picks it
up, confused, his mind reeling.

BOWEN

(to the neighbors)

Hey! Where's Abi? Where's my mom?
Where is she? What's going on?

IN SLOW MOTION − Time slows. The roar of the fire
fades into a dull hum. Bowen notices the neighbors aren't
looking at the house. They are looking past it, toward the
trees. He runs to the back, dropping to his knees. Tears
stream down his face, the slipper clenched tight against his
chest.

LUCAS

(muffled)

Bowen! What have you done? Bowen!

Long gray hair drifts in the autumn wind. His mother's face is frozen in torture, blood dried around her nose, ears, and eyes. Her white nightgown is torn and muddy and stained with blood. A sign on her chest marks her for the world to see: TRAITOR! Her bony feet dangle inches above a bed of golden leaves.

Her beaten

body

swings

slowly,

lifelessly,

from   the   tree.

Pastor Lucas grips Bowen's shoulder, his eyes horrified beneath his tiny round glasses.

LUCAS

Bowen! You hear me? United Worlds
soldiers did this. They came looking for
you. Were you at a hacker tournament?

Bowen stares at Pastor Lucas without blinking, his eyes wild, trying to understand, to process what's happening. He tried to save her honestly. But honesty failed. Failure turned to desperation, desperation turned to crime, and the crime became her death sentence.

> LUCAS
>
> Bowen! What did you do? The founder
> of the United Worlds gave the order.
> Rhea. The soldiers... They accused your
> mom of treason?

Bowen is frozen by the sight of his dead mother.

> LUCAS
>
> They were shouting at your mom, asking
> for some key. A key that belongs to this
> famous person, Rhea. You stole it? You
> stole from the founder of the United
> Worlds? But why?

Pastor Lucas stops, breathless, struggling to reconcile the boy he knows with this madness.

> LUCAS
>
> I don't... This is...
> (shaking Bowen)
> Bowen! You hear me? Answer me!

> BOWEN
> (whispering)
> I-I didn't steal anything.

Bowen stands, dizzy, fire reflecting on his shiny, sweaty face, twisting with rage and guilt and pain.

He slams his backpack to the ground, screaming. The VR headset tumbles out, the screen cracked. He yanks the metallic disc shaped like a Jewish skullcap and throws it into the fire.

FROM BOWEN'S POV (B&W): His mother hangs surrounded by fire embers, which shine in bright white as he sees in black and white.

EXT. FOREST - NIGHT

Bowen's silhouette whips the forest floor with a thick branch. Fireflies flicker around him, casting a soft, mystical glow in the dark night.

Drenched in sweat and fury, he punishes the ground. He tries to break the world, but only breaks the branch and his own hands.

* * *

At his open-air workshop, a red headlamp cuts through the dark. Bowen hunches over the table, building a hearing device from salvaged radio parts and a baby monitor.

EXT. MOUNTAIN CEMETERY - NIGHT

Two gravediggers work by the flickering yellow-orange glow of lanterns set on the ground. Shovels bite into the earth, piling dirt beside a deepening hole. Crunch. Lift. Thud. Crunch. Lift. Thud.

Bowen watches from afar, hidden behind a thick tree.

When they finish, the men limp away, exhausted shadows disappearing into the night.

Bowen steps out of the trees silently. He plants the hearing device on the tree nearest the open grave.

He stares into the black hole in the ground with glassy eyes. Slowly, he climbs down inside. And lies there... on the cold dirt. He should be the one who's dead. Not his poor mother.

Bowen grabs a handful of grave dirt, clenching it with hate. He slams his fist into the ground, wanting to scream. Instead, he covers his face, sobbing in silence, choking on an unthinkable rage.

INT. VAN - NIGHT

Bowen lies curled up in the back of his mother's van, shivering under two jackets. His face is streaked with dirt and tears. His breath fogs in the freezing air.

EXT. BOWEN'S HOUSE - DAWN

Ashes float in the early light. Remnants of smoke linger.

The rope used to hang Bowen's mother still dangles from the tree, cut clean. Its fibers, once tightly bound together and hidden, are now separated and exposed.

Bowen steps out of the van and disappears into the forest.

EXT. MOUNTAIN CEMETERY - MORNING

Thick fog blurs hundreds of small headstones and a few tall crosses. Autumn leaves carpet the grassy hill. Leafless trees stretch their branches toward the hazy sky like skeleton silhouettes.

The entire small town of Homewood has turned out for the funeral.

Far away, Bowen lies on his stomach behind a headstone. He watches the ceremony through a broken binocular lens, the hearing device pressed to his ear. The fog makes it hard to see.

Bowen swallows hard at the sight of the modest wooden coffin. He forces his gaze away and finds Pastor Lucas. The wind stirs the old man's long black-gray beard and ponytail. He looks troubled, his eyes narrowed behind tiny round glasses, fixed on something. Bowen follows his gaze. Two strangers linger near the edge of the crowd, scanning faces. They look military.

> LUCAS
> Today, we lay Abigail Huxley to rest.
> She was a kind and faithful woman. She
> made Homewood her home. And gave
> it everything she had. I look around and
> see our entire community has shown up.

FROM BOWEN'S POV (B&W): The scenery is more

haunting without colors. He can't take his eyes off the coffin.

> LUCAS (ON HEARING DEVICE)
> We live in an age of temptation, do we
> not? In an age of illusion. A false world,
> a virtual world, that promises a better
> life–

The audio cuts with a static hiss.

> LUCAS (ON HEARING DEVICE)
> People no longer want truth. They want
> the illusion of truth. But –
> (audio cuts)
> –ificial worlds cannot save your soul.
> They're not real. And you know what?
> The biggest problem isn't that United
> Worlds replaces reality. The biggest
> pro–
> (audio crackles)
> people stop caring that it did. And they –

The signal fights a losing battle against the dying battery.

> LUCAS (ON HEARING DEVICE)
> United Worlds is a place where billions
> go to avoid reality. But Abi knew what
> mattered. What the –
> (audio cuts)
> lived by grace. And she died, for

another's sin.

Bowen looks down, a tear rolling down his dirty face. He turns, and a deer is nibbling the grass, not far away.

> LUCAS (ON HEARING DEVICE)
> Our nation has bowed –
> (static hiss)
> hanging American citizens –
> (static hiss)
> sweet Abi –
> (static hiss)
> –cret key –
>
> (static hiss)
> treason. Of –
>
> (static hiss)
> into His true kin–

The device gives one last click and dies.

The deer freezes mid-bite, ears twitching as it looks at Bowen, alarmed.

Biology doesn't define humanity

I chased the cure and made my whole world crash,
my cross lies buried in the pile of ash.
the rope is cut, fibers baring the grief,
now the real is gone, so is my belief.

—Bowen Huxley

Chapter 5
Patterns of the soul

16 min read

Previously...

Bowen was awarded Best Player at the hacker tournament, but the ceremony turned into a massacre when United Worlds soldiers stormed the arena.

General Zeffross shot Bowen, but the U.W. Port disconnected him for staying past his paid time, unintentionally saving his life.

When Bowen returned home, he found his house engulfed in flames, and his mother hanging from a tree. Pastor Lucas revealed the U.W. soldiers had come looking for him because he competed in an illegal hacker tournament, and they accused him of stealing a key that belonged to Rhea, the founder of the United Worlds. An accusation Bowen denies.

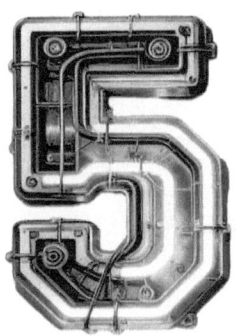

EXT. VAN - MORNING

A beaten-up futuristic van is parked in front of Bowen's burnt cabin, wrapped in colorful flower graphics and religious stickers. One on the rear window declares: "Jesus is my savior."

The van's wipers clear the ashes from the cracked windshield, revealing Bowen behind the wheel. He cries like someone pushed past their limit.

But he forces it back. He won't let himself break. He stares at the crucifix hanging from the rearview mirror, grief turning into fury... and rips it down.

Determination takes over his face. He wipes the tears and the shine beneath his nose, and takes a deep breath.

EXT. HIGHWAY - VAN - DAY

On the rear bumper, a yellow-and-black sticker warns: "Human-driven car. Keep distance."

The van rumbles past a sign reading WELCOME TO NEVADA.

EXT. SCRAP WAREHOUSE - AFTERNOON

Dozens of shoes hang from a power line. Behind them looms a dead billboard with only half a faded ad: "LIVE REAL..."

Bowen parks in an alley next to a warehouse, its fence topped with barbed wire and a crooked sign dangling that reads SCRAP.

A skinny dog sniffs through trash on a wide, unpaved street lined with stripped cars and graffitied campers rotting on flat tires. Beyond the decay, the lake is visible just five blocks down. Across the water, on the far opposite shore of Lake Tahoe, the familiar peaks of his home look small and distant.

The sidewalk is packed with filthy tents, broken glass glittering like tiny diamonds. The street is taken by shady people shuffling past like zombies, many of them glowing from the magenta drug.

A woman in her 50s with messy gray hair pushes a beat-up trolley full of belongings, her body folded into an unnaturally deep hunch.

Bowen walks past an old man with glowing magenta arms and no legs, who is passed out in a wheelchair, baking under the sun. Beside him, two kids, 10 and 12 years old, press patches of magenta liquid to their skinny arms. The ink crawls under their skin like living circuits, lighting up briefly before dissolving into the blood.

INT. SCRAP WAREHOUSE - CONTINUOUS

Towering heaps of discarded tech, rusted metal, and half-dismantled machinery clutter the aisles of a vast, dimly lit warehouse.

ENZO, a 71-year-old U.W. Army veteran who hates the U.W., sits behind the counter. His wrinkled face is framed by a wild beard and stringy, thinning hair. A thick, hand-rolled cigarette is tucked behind his ear.

He scratches off a fluorescent orange lottery ticket with fat fingers, the wedding ring so tight it's become impossible to remove. He holds the ticket steady with his robotic hand.

Enzo stops scratching the ticket when Bowen enters.

BOWEN

Hey. Enzo, right? I'm Bowen.

Enzo stares at him, narrowing his eyes. He recognizes the face, but Bowen is all dirty and looks like he hasn't slept for days.

ENZO
(smoker voice)
Don't I know you?

BOWEN
I bought a few things here a while back.
(pause)
I'm here for... Don sent me. Don Lee?

Enzo looks him up and down. Bowen looks exhausted but restless.

ENZO
Are you okay there, kid?

Bowen clenches his jaw and forces a nod. Enzo narrows his eyes slightly, studying Bowen. *Will this skinny kid cause trouble?*

Enzo rises, tall as a basketball player, long robotic legs powering him up. Intimidating. He glances at the door and through the window to see if there is someone else with him. Or following him.

Bowen trails him down an aisle overflowing with discarded objects reclaiming their value. He grabs a metallic brain-computer-interface disc shaped like a Jewish skullcap, identical to the one he threw into the fire. He runs his thumb over the cold sensors, staring at the vintage device with pure admiration.

Enzo clears his throat loudly, and Bowen puts it back

on the shelf.

At a dead end, Enzo slides a shelf aside with his robotic arm. His robotic legs hiss as they compress, lowering him to the floor. He pulls up a section of the carpet, revealing a secret trapdoor.

They climb down a squeaky wooden ladder into a dark basement glowing with green lights. Seven smuggled lifepods from South America line up in a semicircle, all occupied except for one with a transparent protective cover. Large industrial fans churn the heavy air, fighting the heat.

Enzo switches on a military-grade radio and sets it back on the desk.

> ENZO
> (flapping his shirt to cool off)
> The ventilation system broke the other
> day, but don't worry, I'll fix it.
> (pointing to the floor)
> Watch the tubes.

Enzo opens a drawer on a round table laced with tubes that feed into every lifepod. He takes out an empty canister shaped like a fire extinguisher, and replaces it with another one filled with purple liquid. He twists the valve open.

> ENZO
> I'm taking you in only 'cause Don here
> vouched for you. This is a safe place, and
> it stays that way, alright?
> (uncovering the empty pod)
> That's yours.

Bowen shakes Enzo's robotic hand and nods his thanks.

INT. THERMAL BAR - NIGHT

The walls are living canvases with psychedelic visuals. Colorful abstract images morph hypnotically, crashing like chaotic ocean waves.

People drink and smoke, their avatars glowing as if seen through a thermal camera: a shifting spectrum of fuchsia, purple, red, orange, green, and blue. Their faces blur in the heat-glow, perfect for anonymity. Only the avatars have this effect; the rest of the bar looks normal.

In a secluded booth, Don and Bowen drink electric blue liquor and beer. Don pours two shots and gives one to Bowen, whose face glows with a more intense orange-red than Don's.

> DON
>
> Why did you choose this place, man? I can't see your face.

Bowen downs a shot of blue liquor, chases it with beer, and immediately pours another shot.

> DON
>
> I'm glad you're back.

Bowen sips beer and stays silent.

> DON
>
> Hey, you okay?

> BOWEN
>
> (takes a shot)
>
> Where can I get a gun?

> DON
>
> Wow. What? A gun? Here? Nah, man, only soldiers have guns. I mean, I can make you one, but it won't kill. It's not the bullet that kills. It's the software inside the bullet.

BOWEN

Is that why people get seizures?

DON

The code in the bullet tells your brain
to release a lotta glutamate. We all got
glutamate in our brains. It helps, you
know? But too much of it? And it fries
your fucking brain.

(pause)

What were you planning to do with a
gun anyway?

Bowen scratches his head, looking away. The hot orange
glow of his face is cut by dark, cold trailing lines of tears,
cooling his skin.

DON

Bowen, you okay? What's wrong?

BOWEN

(grimly)

It's my fault. I messed up. She begged me
not to go. Not to come here to this fake
world. She said it was dangerous. And I
didn't...

(swallows hard)

Can't believe she's gone.

Don understands immediately. Knowing how sick Bowen's mother was, he stays silent, letting his friend find the strength to continue.

BOWEN

My mom. She's...

(shaking head)

Rhea? You know Rhea?

DON

Rhea? Wait. You mean, Rhea, the founder of the United Worlds?

(Bowen nods)

Yeah, of course. She's a psychopath. Looks like a teenager, but she's probably a hundred. What about her?

BOWEN

She...

(exhales violently)

Rhea killed my mom. Her soldiers did.

Don stays silent in shock. The news of the illness is one thing, but a murder is something he never expected.

DON

...I'm so sorry, Bo.

BOWEN

How can they do something like that,

huh? It was a tournament. For fuck's
sake, a stupid tournament. Doesn't hurt
anyone. And they go and kill an innocent,
sick old woman... just to get me? Does
that make sense to you? Huh?

Bowen slams another shot. Don gives him a refill.

> BOWEN
> And you know what else doesn't make
> any sense? Pastor Lucas... you know
> what he told me?

Bowen downs another and chugs the beer, his throat
briefly turning deep blue.

> BOWEN
> So he said the United Worlds soldiers
> were asking my mom about a key. A key
> that belongs to Rhea. They think I stole
> it.
> (scoffs)
> Can you believe that shit? I'm telling you.
> These people...

> DON
> He said they were looking for a key?
> Like, a key for what?

BOWEN
(pouring two shots)
Who knows?! They've spent too much
time in this fuckin' illusion, they don't
know what's real anymore.
(drinks the shot)
Can I have one?

Bowen mimics taking a drag, his fingertips glowing hot
yellow against his lips. Don slides the cigarette pack and
lighter across the table. An ashtray materializes between
them.

DON
But how did they track you down?

BOWEN
(lights a smoke, shrugs)
The portal closed. You know, the one you
used to escape the maze. I was trapped...
And they shot me. The General. He shot
me in the fuckin' face.
(coughs yellow-orange clouds)
I should be dead, you know? But the
port disconnected me just in time for not
paying. For not having enough funds. I
don't think they realized they saved me.

DON

Mhm... so I hate to say it, man, but... that's it. If you don't go through customs to leave the United Worlds, your avatar stays where you were. So your avatar stayed in the maze. And you know, avatars carry metadata. Pod info, location, who you are...

As the truth sinks in, erratic purple patches bloom on Bowen's chest.

BOWEN

I can't believe I won't see her again. Ever since she got so sick, I... I had these thoughts. These thoughts of losing her. But I don't know. I thought I could save her, somehow. That she would get well and things would go back to normal. And now that she's...

(pause)

You don't know, Don. She was... She didn't go peacefully. The illness... She would've slipped away in her sleep. I researched it. But this?

(takes a shot)

Sorry I'm laying all this on you. This blue

liquor makes me...

> DON
> Don't be sorry. You can talk to me. Go on.

> BOWEN
> I-I feel this coldness in my chest. Even here in VR I can feel it. It's like an ice bomb went off inside me.
> (pulls his jacket hood up)
> She was all I had. I never met her parents. I...
> (swallows hard)
> I never even met my dad. And that's fine. Don't care about it anymore.
> (chugs beer, sighs)
> It's hard to think I can't talk to her again, you know?

A woman walks past, leaving brief trails of reddish-orange heat.

> DON
> Yeah... Unfortunately, I do know.
> (pause)
> My daughter Annie. She's in a coma.

BOWEN

Don... Fuck. I didn't... I'm sorry.

DON

If she were older, I could upload her. That would cure her. But she's only five.

BOWEN

..."Cure her?" That would kill her.

DON

I already told ya, man. It kills their biological body, but it uploads their consciousness. The person is uploaded.

BOWEN

...But Don... That wouldn't be her.

DON

Oh, c'mon, man. Sorry, but don't be a purist.

BOWEN

A purist? You called me that before. What's that?

DON

Purists treat uploads as if they aren't human. Think they're better than them just 'cause uploads don't have bio bodies. As if that matters.

(points to his chest)

Well, you can't see it here, but my shirt says "we are all human." There's so much backlash against uploads, it's insane. You know they can't vote? Even their families, their *own families*, discriminate against them. Treat them like sub-humans or worse. They're stuck in the old ways, man. Biology doesn't define humanity.

BOWEN

...But they're not real people. Like, I mean... You cannot upload the soul, don't you think?

DON

We're evolved monkeys, Bo. What soul are you talking about? Consciousness, what you call soul, is nothing more than patterns firing in the brain. Memories, feelings... The way one thought leads to another. A strange loop of patterns referring to themselves, monitoring themselves, changing themselves.

(leaning in)

Yeah, you know, very complex shit, but you don't need flesh for that. Who cares if those patterns fire in something biological or artificial? They're still the same thing. Think of it this way, if you'd like. They're the patterns of the soul.

Bowen shakes his head and smokes.

DON

What? Do you know how they upload minds? You know that it's gradual? They go cell by cell, making all the connections you have, and build a virtual brain that's exactly the same as the biological one.

BOWEN

But Don... it's a copy. If it's not the exact same brain, it can't be the exact same person, don't you think?

DON

You know what? Brains change over time, right? Would you say the "you" from 5 years ago isn't still "you?"

(chuckles)

I'd actually argue the "you" after the

upload is even more "you" than the one
from 5 years ago.

Bowen is intrigued by this refreshing perspective. He slams another shot, rocking in his chair, dizzy. That blue liquor is too strong.

Don gets a call and activates a polarized capsule.

A young woman who looks like a Hindu goddess materializes as a hologram, glowing to signal she's not really there. She has hazel eyes and large silver earrings. An ornate silver headpiece sits like a crown, its central pendant resting on her forehead.

Don and Bowen lock eyes, a silent charge of anticipation passing between them.

Chapter 6
Inside his consciousness

28 min read

Previously...

Bowen traveled to the illegal port Don uses.

Inside the United Worlds, he confided in Don about the pain of losing his mother. Don revealed his own tragedy. His daughter is in a coma, and he believes uploading her is the only cure. When Bowen argued the soul cannot be uploaded, Don pushed back, saying the soul is nothing more than patterns firing in the brain. Uploading is a gradual process, happening cell by cell, building a virtual brain identical to the biological one.

The meeting ended when Don received a call from a mysterious woman resembling a Hindu goddess.

Neurons fire in rhythm with electronic music beautifully blended with piano. A symphony of glowing neural activity.

INT. MÖBIUS OPS CENTER - NIGHT

Loba's fingers dance across the keys of a long-tail piano, her golden-yellow wolf eyes following the music on the sheet. Black wolf ears rise through her long, dark curls. Behind her, the U.W. flag hangs beside the Möbius strip.

Möbius headquarters is a massive repurposed airplane hangar, big enough to fit several commercial planes. The back is packed with workstations. The front opens into a game area with pool and ping pong tables, and a training ring.

Don and Bowen materialize at the hangar doorway.

Beside them stands VAISHNAVI, the woman who looks like a Hindu goddess.

The guys are engrossed with how cool this is when Bowen gets knocked down. He spins, eyes wide. General Zeffross. Bowen throws a punch, but Zeffross vanishes, reappearing inside the ring next to J.S., who is laughing at him.

> VAISHNAVI
> Sorry about that. J.S. trains fighting a
> simulation of the General.

J.S. is tall and athletic, his face painted in tribal war style, the kind that intimidates enemies and friends alike. Four muscular arms complete his imposing frame.

> DON
> And the arms?

> VAISHNAVI
> He trained his brain to fight with four.
> (to the Möbius crew)
> Everyone, a moment please. We got new
> prospects: Don and Bowen.

The crew ignores her, dozens of people focused on their screens.

> VAISHNAVI
> Hey! I said we have new prospects.

Loba stops playing the piano, and everyone stops working

to look at V.

> J.S.
>
> Oh, c'mon. Are we that desperate?

> VAISHNAVI
>
> What? They solved the steganography
> challenge in the last tournament.

People are impressed. Loba, arms crossed, not so much.

> J.S.
> (to Don and Bowen)
>
> Oh! Okay! Congratu-fuckin-lations,
> whatever-your-names-are.
> (to Vaishnavi)
> So just for one good hack, huh? Really?
> They might be Rhea's spies as far as we
> know.

Don bursts into laughter. J.S.'s eyes widen, wild. He can't believe this little guy just laughed at him. He marches straight toward him, face twisting in rage, murder in his eyes. All four hands twitch, getting ready for a beatdown.

> DON
>
> Wow, hey, hey. Sorry, chief. I didn't
> mean to. It's just...
> (J.S. keeps coming)
> If you knew us, you'd find it funny too,

man. We are not Rhea's spies, okay?

(J.S. closes the gap)

Chief. C'mon, Chief...

(J.S. raises his fists)

Hey, wait! Rhea killed his mom, okay?

J.S. stops the punch, so close his fists reflect in Don's round yellow lenses. He lowers his arms and shifts his glare to Bowen, whose frown deepens with the sting of his friend's betrayal.

No one knows how to react. Don's face silently pleads with Bowen: *forgive me, man.*

J.S.

Rhea killed your mother?

Bowen's jaw tightens, his lips pressed together. Don waits for him to answer, but when he realizes Bowen will not, he steps in.

DON

Yeah, well, her soldiers did. And his mom
was innocent. Rhea's fucking crazy, man.
You all know that better than anyone.

Bowen turns to leave, but Vaishnavi stops him.

VAISHNAVI

Look, no disrespect, J.S., but I've been
doing this for a long time to recognize

talent. And someone with that kind of
talent? Not a spy.

(to Loba)

You know, we need a good cryptographer
since...

Loba touches her black wolf ears, her golden-yellow eyes
fixed on Bowen, trying to decipher him. There is grief and
anger in his eyes. Bowen stares back, trying to decipher her.
She is terrifying.

LOBA

What do you all say? Should we trust V
and give 'em a chance?

Folks show support, nodding and giving a thumbs-up.
Loba smiles at J.S. with open arms. *There's nothing I can do.*
He glares back.

DON

(shaking Loba's hand)

Hey Loba, I'm Don. Big fan. This is
Bowen.

VAISHNAVI

All right, shall we?

As Vaishnavi explains, an interactive 3D board shows
intel and pictures from Rhea's Secret Council.

VAISHNAVI

Okay, so, this is all the intel we've
gathered over the years. As you can see,
this didn't come easy.

(pause)

Find something valuable on one of the
targets, and you're in. You'll be part of
Möbius. Got it?

The two outsiders eye each other – *harder than we
thought* – but clasp hands, accepting the challenge.

LOBA

All right, guys. Happy hacking.

They interact with the 3D board, fingers sliding through
the cards as they analyze intel, looking for cracks, looking for
ways to get more information about Rhea and her Council.

Bowen grabs a pie chart that shows the voting power
distribution in the United Worlds, which has four slices:
MYSTERY KEY holds 60% of Tores; RHEA, 20%; RHEA'S
SECRET COUNCIL, 10%; THE PEOPLE, 10%. He isolates
the slice of RHEA'S SECRET COUNCIL, and makes it larger.

A list of names unfolds. They are titans of all the
major industries: healthcare, banking, technology, media &
entertainment. Beside each name is listed how much Tores
and money each one has.

At the top of the list, with the most number of Tores,

sits WARNER, a shady, self-made trillionaire in his 30s with a gaze that unsettles. The notes in his profile highlight two details: he is Rhea's boyfriend, and he is obsessed with VR games. Bowen grabs Warner's game list and sends it to his personal screen.

> BOWEN
> Command: scan vulnerabilities in these
> games.

> J.S.
> Pfft, oh yeah. We didn't try that.

A message appears on Bowen's screen: "No known vulnerabilities to exploit."

J.S. smirks, thinking they don't have a chance of passing this test.

Bowen reads through a list of database versions, and isolates one of the games.

> BOWEN
> This one uses a very old version.
> (proudly)
> My expertise is in old tech.

> J.S.
> (sarcastically)
> Oh, really? You don't say. That's exactly
> what we were looking for.

Bowen types, hits ENTER, and a message flashes in red: "ERROR. Terminated signal." Types. ENTER. ERROR. Types. ENTER. ERROR.

J.S. laughs, turning his back to return to the ring.

> BOWEN
> (typing)
> This is a good error, actually. Look, if I
> send billions of bytes in a string to the
> API, it lets me hide prompt commands.
> See? I can trick the AI agent into giving
> me user data. I can get Warner's data.

J.S.'s smirky face turns dead serious. When Vaishnavi grins at him, he flips her off with all four hands.

> J.S.
> Fuck off.

Everyone gathers around, some with mouths open, others smiling, enjoying Bowen's mad skills. Loba raises an eyebrow.

Bowen hits ENTER and waits...

AWAITING RESPONSE FROM API...

Will it work?

ROWS MATCHED: 1

Bowen throws his hands up in victory. Warner's lifepod details stream across his screen. ID, model, firmware version, region. It's all there.

DON
(shaking Bowen)
Man, no fuckin' way! What?
(laughing)
You got his pod info!

Don and Bowen clasp hands.

BOWEN
Look, isn't this beautiful? The same code
that made the program work well in the
past, is what makes it flawed now. 'Cause
it didn't adapt to technical changes. How
fucking poetic is that?

Surprised, Loba nods to V, who shoots back a look: *told
ya.*

LOBA
Okay, Möbius, listen up. We can finally
start active recon. V, put sniffers in all
the ports. Tell me if something useful
gets in his network.
(to others)
Brute force the hash password. He might
use it for other things.

Loba taps Bowen's shoulder and slides in next to him.

BOWEN
(in disbelief)
System's been up for 288 days?

LOBA
I know, right? No one wants to leave the
Worlds. Not even to reboot their pods.
(naughty smile)
Better for us...

They hack together, shoulder to shoulder, surrounded by glowing screens. Their fingers move in sync, a silent rhythm establishing itself between them.

Loba points at a line of code, and they share a laugh. Only hackers would get it.

She glances at his screen and nods, impressed. Bowen hides a smile.

Their fingers freeze over the keys. They lock eyes, a spark of anticipation between them. It's a big moment. His fingertip rests on ENTER, but he doesn't press it. He hesitates. Loba offers a small nod, and he commits. ENTER.

Lines of code flood the screen like a waterfall running in reverse.

ACCESS GRANTED

The hangar erupts in cheers. People congratulate Loba and Bowen, hands clapping their shoulders. They've hacked Warner, and now they can see and hear everything through his eyes and ears.

They lean closer to the screen, peering through Warner's eyes.

EXT. GOLDEN GATE PARK - DAY - MEMORY

FROM WARNER'S POV: On stage, Warner stands with a group of fancy people dressed for a gala. They glow because they're not part of the memory, just in the memory, observing.

Rhea, 35, much older than we've seen her before, but just as beautiful, commands the podium in the heart of the park, surrounded by lush greenery and towering trees, giving a speech to a sea of people on the open meadow. Behind her, two United Worlds banners hang in tall drapes, their dark blue and black stripes running vertically.

The people in the crowd lift signs and banners reading BIG TECH OUT! FREEDOM NOW! BIG TECH SPIES. Many of them have images of Rhea portrayed as a revolutionary icon, her striking red-and-white hair and vivid green eyes demanding attention.

> RHEA
>
> Big corporations created virtual prisons,
> tracking our every move. Trapping us in
> their reality. Well, you know what? It's
> time to break free!

The crowd roars, a wave of sound crashing against the

stage.

> RHEA
>
> I'm happy to announce, after endless
> negotiations with the United States and
> the United Nations...
>> (pause)
> The United Worlds is now recognized as
> an independent, sovereign country!

The park erupts, flags waving frantically.

> RHEA
>
> And let me tell you. We're doing things
> differently this time.

Quick glitches flicker through the memory, less than a second each. In them, a man stands at the podium instead of Rhea, giving the exact same speech.

> RHEA
>
> In the United Worlds, we govern
> ourselves. No more politicians
> representing us. We all know how that
> story ends, don't we?

She smiles. A ripple of knowing laughter moves through the audience.

> RHEA
>
> Any citizen of the United Worlds can

propose laws, and everyone can vote on them using Tores, our digital token that guarantees both equality and anonymity. One person. One Tore. One vote. In our country,

> (raises her fist)

the people are in charge.

Thousands of fists pump in the air. The memory stutters again, and for a split second, the man stands there instead of Rhea, fist raised in triumph.

> RHEA
> So come live with us in the first *direct* democracy in history! Join the United Worlds!

The crowd goes wild.

INT. MÖBIUS OPS CENTER - NIGHT

> LOBA
> Her husband gave that famous speech.
> She clearly tweaked the memory to make herself look like the hero.

Bowen stares at the screen, confused. But not by the glitch. Standing behind Rhea is a U.W. General in her 30s. She looks like his mother, only much younger. Bowen frowns, leaning closer. *A relative?*

EXT. GOLDEN GATE PARK - DAY - MEMORY

A white-gloved BUTLER materializes as a hologram and nods to Warner.

> WARNER
> (to fancy guests)
> Duty calls, I'm afraid. But please, keep admiring Rhea's museum. Remember, these are her personal memories. You are reliving our great nation's history through the eyes of the woman who made it all happen.
> (bows his head)
> It was a privilege sharing one of the most important moments with you all. Enjoy.

INT. CASTLE - NIGHT

Warner follows the butler through an opulent ballroom packed with powerful people dressed for a gala. Massive light-spheres float overhead, casting a soft glow on the crowd.

> LOBA (VOICE OVER)
> Oh shit. This is Rhea's castle.

Warner trails the butler into a private library with exquisite futuristic furniture and art. The butler stops at a shelf, takes a thick red book with gold on the page edges, and leaves it open on the floor. Putting his hand on Warner's shoulder, he steps on the book, and they're transported to a cave tunnel lit by neon purple and yellow lights.

They arrive at an ethereal luminescence waterfall, which opens like a curtain, revealing a UNITED WORLDS SOLDIER heavily armored.

The soldier rings a bell, and waits...

A red light on the stone wall turns green, and Warner walks through the wall.

INT. CASTLE SECRET CHAMBER - CONTINUOUS

Warner steps through the wall and finds himself at the top of a grand staircase. Below lies a futuristic lounge framed by large, angled glass windows. They offer a panoramic view of the ocean and a secluded tropical beach under a starry sky.

Rhea's Council is here. Some sit on a curved, dark leather sofa centered around a circular fire pit with a warm flame. Others gather at the sleek white bar, illuminated by shelves packed with glowing bottles.

General Zeffross stands apart. He isn't wearing a helmet, his eyes all white, no pupils, no irises, making his dark face unreadable. He watches the grand staircase, waiting for Rhea.

INT. MÖBIUS OPS CENTER - CONTINUOUS

Everyone looks at each other with wide eyes, stunned.

                    LOBA

V, help me set up the Possession.

                 VAISHNAVI

On it.

                    BOWEN

The Possession? What's that?

                    LOBA

It's a program to hijack his avatar.
Control it from the inside.

                 VAISHNAVI

Like a demon possession. Way more
powerful than a DeepFake. We lock the
victim in his dreams while we use his
avatar.
        (off Bowen's impressed face)
I know, right? Loba's always inventing
wild shit. Get used to it.

                    BOWEN

Can I be the one controlling Warner's
avatar?

                    J.S.

Yeah, right. No fucking way.

LOBA

Sorry... Bowen, right? You're not ready.

BOWEN

So, I do the hack, and you take over?
That's how things work around here?

LOBA

Hey. C'mon. We hacked it together.

BOWEN

Yeah, 'cause I got his pod info.

V shoots Loba a look: *fair point.* Loba touches her wolf
ears, considering.

LOBA

If they kill you in his avatar, you die for
real. You know that, right? Your pod
will stimulate your brain as if you were
Warner. So if he gets shot, you die.

Bowen shrugs.

LOBA

'Kay, but don't fuck it up.

J.S.

What? This is bullshit! C'mon!

A red teleport ring burns into the floor.

> VAISHNAVI
> (to Bowen)
> Step here. Hurry.

Bowen steps onto the teleport base, nervous, the light washing over him.

> LOBA
> (to Bowen)
> Listen. You'll feel like you're him. But also still you. It's weird. You might get dizzy, but don't panic, okay?

> VAISHNAVI
> Channel two created. It's ready.

One screen plays Warner's old dreams, while another broadcasts his live feed, showing exactly what he is seeing now at Rhea's chamber.

Vaishnavi's control panel looks like a DJ's, filled with knobs, faders, and buttons.

> VAISHNAVI
> I'll make the swap. Ready?

The moment Bowen nods, she slides two faders apart, dissolving him.

INT. CASTLE SECRET CHAMBER - NIGHT

Bowen hijacks Warner's avatar, making him stumble and

crash to the ground, barely missing the circular fire pit beside the sofa. The room goes silent. All eyes turn to him.

> WARNER
>
> I'm fine.

Warner tilts his head, as Bowen is surprised by his new voice.

He scrambles up and staggers to the white bar, needing to look busy. He presses a button and a beer materializes. His eyes sweep the room every few seconds, alert for danger. Fewer than a dozen people fill the room, but they're the most powerful in the United Worlds. Only Rhea is missing.

Warner winces. Bowen feels a sudden wave of nausea. Something is wrong. Without moving his lips, just using his thoughts, he talks to Loba.

> BOWEN (VOICE OVER)
>
> What the fuck is this?

> LOBA (V.O.)
>
> You okay, Bowen?

> BOWEN (V.O.)
>
> I... don't feel like myself.

> LOBA (V.O.)
>
> You're inside his consciousness.

> BOWEN (V.O.)
> ...I know this place. I remember being here.

> LOBA (V.O.)
> That's him. His memories.

> BOWEN (V.O.)
> They feel like my memories.

INT. MÖBIUS OPS CENTER - CONTINUOUS

> LOBA
> I know. Hang on. Adjusting now.

Loba signals V, who slides faders on the control panel to adjust how much of Warner's consciousness is shared.

> LOBA
> Better?

On the live feed, Warner looks down at his hand and makes a *so-so* wobble.

> LOBA
> You're doing fine. Don't fight it.

INT. CASTLE SECRET CHAMBER - CONTINUOUS

Warner's hand trembles slightly as he takes a sip. The beer tastes awful. He smells it and doesn't like the scent either. He frowns, confused. *That's a first.*

Warner's eyes find an immense textured painting of a country road surrounded by pink-orange poppies. The long dirt road disappears into the horizon, pulling you into the painting. An artwork label on the wall reads: "**Anselm Kiefer**, *Bohemia Lies by the Sea*, 1996."

A memory flashes FROM WARNER'S POV: He is inside that painting, kissing passionately with Rhea in the poppy fields.

The memory ends.

Warner runs his fingers over the thick painting, unsure of what he just had.

Another memory flashes FROM WARNER'S POV: Inside a vault, he massages Rhea's shoulders as she sits before a floating screen, using all her Tores to vote on new laws.

The memory ends.

Warner takes another sip, but the beer is disgusting. As he turns to get something else from the bar, a hand lands on his shoulder. He freezes, afraid to turn.

> WOMAN'S VOICE
> (whispering right in his ear)
> Art reveals deeper truths about the
> world. Don't you agree, honey?

Warner's body shivers. He turns... and Rhea is right there, inches away. She is exactly like the posters, striking red-and-white hair, freckled face, barely out of her teens. She smiles, seductive, her green gaze cutting sharp. She's dressed in all black, like a widow.

Rhea leans in with her eyes closed, trying to kiss Warner, but he pulls away, dodging the kiss.

> LOBA (V.O.)
> What are you doing? Kiss her.

A memory flashes FROM BOWEN'S POV (B&W): His mother, Abi, hangs dead, surrounded by fire embers that shine in bright white as he sees in black and white.

The memory ends.

> RHEA
> What? You're still angry at me?

Warner looks away, then back to Rhea. *She knows*. Why else would she ask that? He grips the glass and takes a nervous sip.

> LOBA (V.O.)
> Kiss her. You're gonna blow it.

How do you kiss the person who killed your mother?

> RHEA
> Hon, what's wrong?
> (pointing at Warner's glass)
> Is that...? Are you drinking beer?

She stares, trying to read what's going on with him.

Warner hates beer.

Out of the corner of his eye, Bowen sees General Zeffross heading their way.

LOBA (V.O.)

C'mon Bowen... Kiss her!

Zeffross glares at Warner, who forces a smile and kisses Rhea.

Another memory flashes FROM BOWEN'S POV (B&W): Abi hangs dead in her white nightgown, bruised and covered in black blood.

The memory ends.

Warner pulls away as if he'd been punched in the face.

WARNER

Sorry. I'm not feeling too well.

General Zeffross steps closer, his muscular build facing Rhea.

ZEFFROSS

Sorry to interrupt, boss. But everyone's
here. Dr. Holland is ready. Should we?

Rhea doesn't answer. She can't take her eyes from Warner, studying his weird behavior. Zeffross picks it up, sensing the tension. Finally, Rhea turns to the room. She raises a hand and snaps her fingers, the sound cracking like a whip.

The room freezes. Conversations die instantly. Rhea

beckons everyone like dogs, and the most powerful people in the United Worlds scramble to obey. She walks to the center, carrying herself like she owns everything and everyone.

Bowen spots Zeffross' handgun, attached to his belt.

> RHEA
>
> I wanna start by recognizing the incredible progress we've made over the years. When we founded the United Worlds, it wasn't easy, remember? Hackers were destroying–

Warner inches closer, his hand brushing Zeffross' belt.

> RHEA
>
> –people's lives. Stealing their memories, exposing them to the public. Even I was a victim. One of the worst moments in my life.

Warner's fingers find the retention strap. He flicks it open. *Click*. It's soft, but to Bowen, it sounds like a gunshot. He holds his breath. Zeffross doesn't react.

> RHEA
>
> But we've restored order. We've made the Worlds a better place.

She applauds her Council, congratulating them for the achievement they have made in securing the future. They join in, applauding themselves for the peace they have restored.

RHEA

And tonight... tonight is special. For
decades, we've been working on a secret
project. Project Remedy.

Warner reaches for the handgun, his fingertips on
the handle, but Zeffross moves away, heading toward the
staircase. Warner grabs nothing but air.

DR HOLLAND proudly walks down the staircase. He
is a visionary neuroscientist in his 40s, radiating the quiet
arrogance of a man about to change history. Behind him,
United Worlds soldiers escort three prisoners in blood-red
jumpsuits. They move sluggishly, heavily drugged, their chains
rattling with every step.

PRISONER #1 stumbles but catches himself. He is 35,
with a blue beard and red hair that makes him stand out. He
holds his chin high, glaring at the room, defiant.

PRISONER #2 is a woman, strikingly tall. She looks down,
defeated, her long gray hair covering her face. PRISONER #3
is barely more than a girl, her head shaved and face covered
in tattoos. She presses her trembling hands together, offering
a silent plea for mercy to anyone who will look at her.

RHEA

Technology allows us to control all
senses, right? But why stop there?

She grabs PRISONER #1 by the jaw, her grip iron-tight. She forces him to look at her.

> RHEA
>
> Wouldn't life be much easier and better
> if we didn't have to fight and disagree all
> the time?
> (pause)
> The problem is that people can't control
> their negative thoughts. It's a sickness.

Dr. Holland opens a silver case containing three syringes filled with glowing yellow liquid. He gives one to Rhea and one to General Zeffross. He keeps the third.

> RHEA
>
> What if we could cure them? Change
> their minds?
> (smiles)
> I mean, literally change their minds?

Without warning, they spin the prisoners around, and stab the syringes into their necks. All three prisoners fall to the ground, screaming and twitching in pain.

Transparent capsules materialize, swallowing each prisoner whole. The glass muffles their agony to a dull hum.

No one enjoys watching this. Even Rhea looks away, feeling uncomfortable. But there is a hint of satisfaction at the corner of her mouth. She believes this is the price of progress, the price of building a better world.

Brain maps float above the capsules, displaying progress bars.

RECONFIGURATION: 5%...

The maps morph and twist, as new neuronal connections are made. Their brains rearrange with unbearable pain.

Inside a prisoner's brain, neurons glow with messy but beautiful sparks, an orchestra of light. Connections between neurons shatter and reform into new patterns.

INT. MÖBIUS OPS CENTER - CONTINUOUS

The Möbius crew stares at the live feed, horrified by the torture and the terrifying reality of this new technology.

> VAISHNAVI
> People are gonna freak out when they see this.

> J.S.
> You still think they give a shit? They'll say it's fake, like always.

INT. CASTLE SECRET CHAMBER - CONTINUOUS

The brain maps of PRISONER #1 and #3 turn into red skull icons, confirming their deaths. Rhea shoots Dr. Holland a withering glare.

PRISONER #2's tracker turns green.

RECONFIGURATION:

100% COMPLETE

The woman passes out. Her gray hair spills in all directions as the chains fade away. Dr. Holland rushes to her and shakes her. No response. He eyes Rhea, worried. *Zero out of three?*

But with her back to everyone except Rhea, PRISONER #2 rises, nearly three heads taller, and gives a military salute.

> PRISONER #2
> (whispering to Rhea)
> I'll get you the key.

Rhea grins and taps the prisoner's chest. Dr. Holland can breathe again, shoulders sagging.

General Zeffross applauds. After a stunned silence, the others follow, still shocked by what they just saw.

> RHEA
> You've just witnessed the future. No more elaborate techniques to influence people. No more prisons. No more executions. No more
> (lowering her voice)
> torture. We can save people's lives by changing who they are. Do you realize how powerful that is? We can take
> (pointing to PRISONER #2)

traitors and make 'em loyal citizens.
Citizens who actually contribute. That's
why we call it... the Remedy.

As the room erupts in applause, Rhea pretends to be modest, but her eyes give her away.

RHEA
(pointing to the two dead)
It's not ready yet, obviously. We're still
working out some minor issues, but
we're close. Right, doctor?

Dr. Holland nods quickly, scared.

RHEA
Now, if you'll excuse me, I need to catch
up with my old friend.
(to PRISONER #2)
Akira, it's been, what? 20 years since
we last talked? No, wait. I should know
better. 18 years.

Rhea walks toward the bar with AKIRA, the only prisoner who survived.

Warner's eyes drift back to Zeffross' handgun. It's right there, unsecured. This is it, probably the best chance he'll ever get to kill them, to avenge his mother's violent death. He reaches for the gun.

LOBA (V.O.)

Bowen! For fuck's sake. Whatcha doing?
Follow the scientist. We need access to
that program.

Loba's voice startles Bowen, and for a moment he doubts. Should he go through with his plan for revenge or follow the scientist? He looks at Rhea's back. He grits his teeth and makes his choice. He ignores Loba and creeps up from behind the General, reaching for the grip.

But Zeffross suddenly spins and bumps into him. The General scowls, his hand instinctively dropping to his holster. Bowen freezes, heart hammering. He's lost the element of surprise.

Warner bows in apology, and rushes up the stairs to catch up with Dr. Holland.

Zeffross stands still, watching Warner run up the steps. His white eyes narrow.

Chapter 7
Artificial nature

21 min read

Previously...

Bowen and Don were invited to try out for Möbius, the famous hacktivist group led by Loba.

During the test, Bowen hacked into a database and extracted critical information about Warner, a powerful member of Rhea's Council. He hijacked Warner's avatar and slipped inside his consciousness while Warner remained trapped in a dream.

Inside her secret chamber, Rhea unveiled the Remedy, a terrifying technology that rewires the human brain by forcing new neural connections, changing who a person is.

INT. CASTLE LIBRARY - CONTINUOUS

Bowen, inside Warner's avatar, hurries after Dr. Holland.

WARNER

Doctor! Doctor!

Dr. Holland stops, clutching his silver case. He looks surprised to be addressed by a Council member. And Rhea's boyfriend, in particular.

WARNER

Hey, wow. That was fascinating.

HOLLAND

Thank you, sir. That's very kind of you.

WARNER

I mean it. You should be very proud. I'd
love to learn more about it. Would you
mind?

Holland's eyes light up. A Council member interested in
his work?

HOLLAND

Councilman, I could talk all day about
this.

INT. NEUROSCIENCE LAB - CONTINUOUS

Dr. Holland leads Warner into a sanctuary of science.
Two long desks face each other, separated by a central aisle
where brains float, displaying neural systems in fluorescent
neon colors. Scientific drawings and math equations scrawl
across the glass walls.

A single neuron cell floats, purple and orange, magnified
to the size of a beach ball for observation.

For a moment, Warner forgets to breathe. Something
about this feels familiar.

A memory flashes FROM A 5-YEAR-OLD BOY'S POV:
He is crouched in the shadows of a dark lab, knees pulled
tight to his chest. He is shaking and crying silently, trying to
make himself small, trying to disappear.

The memory ends.

Warner winces and scratches the back of his neck, uneasy. Was that another of Warner's memories?

HOLLAND

Councilman, are you okay?

Warner forces a smile and nods, shaking off the memory.

At the far corner of the lab, a prisoner lies on a medical bed inside a glass cage. Suspended above, a huge brain rotates, showing the prisoner's brain activity through flowing colors.

Next to the cage, at Dr. Holland's workstation, screens glow with a live map of the prisoner's neural pathways.

HOLLAND

For decades we've collected data from brain activity of everyone in the United Worlds. We've used that to train our AI models. It wasn't easy, you know, but we're now able to rewire the human brain by forcing new neural connections.

WARNER

That changes how a person thinks?

HOLLAND

That changes who they are.

The doctor gets a notification from General Zeffross, making him nervous.

HOLLAND

Uh, for most citizens, this is easy, right?
We control all the ports, all the lifepods.
We can access their brains without any
issues and stimulate them however we
like. They're all in our databases, as you
know.

The doctor logs into the Remedy and selects a random
name. A small-scale avatar appears on the screen, spinning
next to a control panel with personality sliders and buttons.

HOLLAND

So we just log in, select the citizen, and
make the changes we'd like to their
brains. It's that easy. But...

Holland taps PRINT, materializing a syringe filled with
glowing yellow liquid on the desk.

HOLLAND
(proudly showing the syringe)
Aha! These beauties are for those in
illegal ports. The criminals. They're off
the grid, right? Not in our databases. We
can't access their brains by logging into
the system, like we can do for normal
citizens. So we have to find their avatars
and inject them with this. Like we did

with the prisoners. The code is inside
the yellow liquid.

(sighs)

But well... you saw what happened. This
technology is still new, and we need to
keep working on it to make it better.
From the three prisoners, only the
upload survived. We need the Remedy
to be more stable before we can apply it
to everyone.

The doctor gets another message from Zeffross only he
can see: URGENT.

HOLLAND

...I'm sorry. We need to head back.

WARNER

Go ahead. I'll be right there.

Dr. Holland bites his lip, unsure. Warner's expression
hardens into a deep frown, making no effort to hide his
offense.

HOLLAND

Okay, okay. But be careful. Please. This
is my career right here.

Dr. Holland leaves, uneasy and nervous, muttering to
himself, clearly on edge.

The moment the door slides shut, Warner drops the act. He slides into the chair, and his fingers fly across the dashboard.

> WARNER
> (typing fast)
> Loba, I'm planting a backdoor so we can
> figure it out later, okay?

Möbius watches the live feed, tense. Bowen is coding as fast as he can.

> LOBA (V.O.)
> C'mon. This should be quick, Bowen.

Warner raises his eyebrows. *Oh, okay, no pressure.*

He hits ENTER, and the screen flashes: "Your tunnel is established..."

> WARNER
> Boom! Done. Just gotta delete the logs
> and...

As he pulls up the event logs on a screen, the lab door opens.

It's General Zeffross.

Warner hides below the desk.

> ZEFFROSS
> I saw you! What're you doing?

> LOBA (V.O.)
> He doesn't know. Play it cool.

Warner reappears behind the desk. With a sleight of hand, he slips the syringe with yellow liquid into his side pocket.

> WARNER
> Sorry, I hid 'cause... You know... Doc said nobody should see me here. Why are *you* here?

Zeffross doesn't answer. He stands still, the silence making Bowen uncomfortable.

Everything turns red. Siren wails. A sign materializes.

MILITARY LOCKDOWN

Zeffross taps his wrist and a golden rifle materializes in his hands, the selector switch set to KILL. He advances along the desk while Warner backs toward the exit, hands up, edging behind the second desk for cover.

> ZEFFROSS
> Who are you?

INT. MÖBIUS OPS CENTER - CONTINUOUS

> VAISHNAVI
> Bowen, get ready. We're pulling you out.

> LOBA

No, wait. Bowen, it's your call, but if you don't clear the logs, they'll find the backdoor.

> VAISHNAVI

But he's made.

Loba ignores her, engrossed in the live feed.

> VAISHNAVI

Loba!

> LOBA

Love you and all, V, but back off.
> (typing on her dashboard)
He's Rhea's boyfriend, right?

INT. NEUROSCIENCE LAB - CONTINUOUS

Zeffross strides to the glass cage, staring down at the prisoner.

> ZEFFROSS

What was he doing?
> (gets a blank stare)
I'll set you free if you tell me.

The prisoner holds his gaze... and gives him the finger. Zeffross taps OPEN on the workstation console, making the cage vanish, and fires. The prisoner hits the floor, his body thrashing in violent seizures before going still.

Warner tries the door. Locked. Zeffross raises his rifle. Warner freezes, hands up, eyes scanning for options.

> LOBA (V.O.)
> Here, got it! Bowen, you hear me? Warner has invisibility powers. To activate, say "command vanish."

> WARNER
> Command: vanish.

Warner disappears, his avatar becoming invisible.

Zeffross shoots several times, from left to right, covering all possible positions.

At the Möbius center, V and Don exchange worried glances. *Is Bowen dead?* Loba's mouth slightly opens, frozen.

FROM ZEFFROSS POV: The lab is empty. He hears footsteps rushing him from the right and fires to the air non-stop until he gets pushed by an invisible force.

Zeffross trips over the dead prisoner. The rifle clatters to the floor. He scrambles back up, drawing his handgun from his belt, and fires. But the bullet vanishes on impact as the glass cage materializes around him, trapping him inside.

Warner reappears on the other side of the glass, holding Zeffross' golden rifle.

The Möbius crew erupts in cheers.

QUICK SHOT of U.W. soldiers marching down a lab hallway.

Warner goes back to eliminating the logs. His screen reads: "2101 records wiped from Application, System, and Security."

> ### WARNER
> All set!
> (to Zeffross)
> You wanted to know who I am, you piece
> of shit? I'm Bowen Huxley. Your soldiers
> killed my mom, Abigail Huxley.

The General steps back and looks away, thinking. He tucks away his handgun and removes his helmet, shaking his head, denying it. He says something, but no sound escapes the soundproof glass.

> ### WARNER
> Sorry, you wanna say something?

Zeffross nods. Warner taps a button on Dr. Holland's dashboard, making the cage disappear.

> ### ZEFFROSS
> Your mo–

BOOM. Headshot. Zeffross collapses, suffering painful seizures. Above him, the floating brain erupts into a chaotic electric storm, the neurons flaring white-hot, firing at their breaking point.

Through the tremors, he claws for his handgun, aiming with a hand that won't stop shaking. He pulls the trigger wildly, bullets whistling inches past Warner's head, until the glowing pulses in the floating brain finally flicker out into darkness.

Zeffross gives one final, rigid twitch, then goes limp.

Warner's face is mixed with relief and rage and satisfaction. Adrenaline electrifies his body.

He admires the powerful rifle, holding it tight.

LOBA (V.O.)

We're pulling you out now.

WARNER

Will the gun come with me?

> LOBA (V.O.)
>
> Yes. Anything you hold that wasn't Warner's will get transported too.

The doors burst open. Soldiers rush into the lab, carrying black paralyzer rifles. They open fire. Warner drops, eyes open, motionless.

INT. MÖBIUS OPS CENTER - CONTINUOUS

The red teleport ring flares on the floor. Bowen materializes, clutching the golden rifle. The group cheers, swarming him like a hero, except J.S., who stays back, his four arms crossed.

Loba steps forward and slips a Möbius necklace over his head. She grabs him by the shoulders, nodding, impressed.

Don smiles, finding it cool how the legendary Loba is treating his new friend. He stays quiet, not wanting to interrupt. But when Loba turns away to the console, he clasps hands with Bowen, pulling him into a hug.

> DON
>
> Bo, respect, man. You're a badass. Lemme see the gun. I'll try to make replicas.

Shaking, Bowen hands him the rifle. He sits but stands back up. Too much adrenaline running through his body.

LOBA

(to Don, pointing at the gun)

Hey, you need to clean that, okay? It's very important. They can trace it back to us 'cause it wasn't Warner's. Got it? Make sure you clean it well.

Don nods and rushes to an empty workstation. He sets the gun on a round base, and a purple aura rises around it.

LOBA

(to herself)

Command: scan the entire program. I want a detailed report.

A progress bar appears on one of the screens, flashing: ACCESSING ROOT DIRECTORY.

J.S.

A report? We need to encrypt it.

LOBA

No. If we encrypt now, they can recover the weapon. We first need to find all their backups.

(before J.S. can reply)

Look, we don't have much time, but it will take their forensics team at least a day so...

The screens flood with data. Columns of complex code cascade down the monitors like a digital waterfall, scrolling faster than the eye can follow. It is endless.

> VAISHNAVI
> Look at that. The code is huge. Will take hours to go through it all.
> (to Loba)
> Hey, today was a big win. And we've got two new members.

> J.S.
> Two?
> (pointing to Don)
> That guy didn't do shit.

They ignore him. V comes closer to Loba.

> VAISHNAVI
> You know what we should do while we wait, right?

V dances seductively while Loba watches with crossed arms and a serious face. But then she rolls her sad, golden-yellow eyes, giving in with a smile. Now V turns to Bowen.

> VAISHNAVI
> (extending hands to Bowen)
> We're gonna celebrate. C'mon.

She seduces him with her hazel eyes, a beautiful mix

of brown, green, and golden, urging him to join them. Her fuchsia and pink-orange silk kimono flows around her, contrasting beautifully with her darker skin. Beneath it, she wears a patterned bikini top and low-rise pants, revealing a belly button piercing shaped like the Möbius loop.

> BOWEN
> (sitting)
> ...I'll join you later.

V pouts, giving him a playful, disappointed face. She turns to the room, raising her arms.

> VAISHNAVI
> C'mon, Möbius. Follow me.

Everyone follows V, except Don and Loba.

> LOBA
> (to Don)
> Hey, is the gun clean?

> DON
> All clean. Don't worry.

Bowen sits perched on the edge of the seat, staring at the floor. His leg bounces uncontrollably. He is still trembling with adrenaline.

> DON
> Hey man, you okay?

BOWEN

Just need a minute. Go.

DON

(to Loba)

We'll catch up in a few.

BOWEN

No. Go. Seriously. I'm fine. I just need a minute. By myself. Go.

Don hesitates, torn. Loba steps closer and leans over Bowen, her hand settling on his restless knee, stopping the bouncing.

LOBA

Look, life's fucked up. I get it. But we celebrate what we can, you know? We owe it to those who aren't with us anymore.

She squeezes his knee, then stands up. She signals Don to follow. As they walk away, Don looks back. The distant look in Bowen's eyes worries him.

INT. BOWEN'S SPACE STATION

Bowen sits alone at the bar, drinking electric blue liquor, his teary eyes fixed on the giant ringed planet floating outside.

A memory flashes FROM BOWEN'S POV (B&W): His

mother, Abi, hangs dead in a torn, dirty white nightgown, her face covered in so much black blood that it looks like something exploded inside her skull.

The memory ends.

Bowen slams the drink back, burning his throat. A single tear rolls down his cheek. If only he hadn't come to the United Worlds. If only...

He scratches his head. The image of her face won't leave. He scratches harder. And harder. Digging his fingernails in, trying to claw the memory out of his brain.

A soft chime breaks the silence and a magenta notification materializes in midair, glowing against the darkness.

Do you wish to relive happy memories
with your mother?

YES   NO

Bowen stops scratching. He looks around the empty station, the hair on his arms standing up. It's so fucking creepy.

INT. CINEMA - CONTINUOUS

Bowen sinks into a comfy couch, the room falling away around him. A massive screen illuminates his face with a soft white glow.

Title: "Memories."

Sub-title: "Memories make us who we are."

Below, a disclaimer in red: "Note: Memories may be reconstructed and influenced by your imagination."

A library of folders appears, sorted by Date, Person, and Emotion. Bowen's eyes scan all of them. He chews his lip, hesitating to open one labeled REPRESSED. What disturbing memories will he find there? What is his mind trying to hide?

He doesn't have the courage to find out. Not now.

He aims at the screen with his finger and the largest folder, FAVORITES, responds with a glowing white aura to show it is selected.

He taps the empty air and the folder ripples like water. A list of memory clips appears.

As he opens one, the room transforms.

EXT. FOREST - AFTERNOON - MEMORY

FROM BOWEN'S POV: His mother, Abi, is right there. Alive. She is in her 40s, healthy and vibrant, her skin glistening with sweat. It's a hot summer day.

They hike up a steep mountain trail, cutting through the woods, dodging the sunlight that leaks through the canopy.

IN SLOW MOTION – A family of majestic deer appears out of nowhere, thundering past them, inches away, shaking the ground with powerful strides and resonant sounds.

Bowen and Abi look at each other, their mouths open, their eyes saying, *did that really just happen?*

A magenta notification materializes in midair, floating

right in front of his mother's smiling face.

Don sent you a memory

OPEN   DISMISS

Bowen sighs. As he taps OPEN, the forest transforms.

INT. NIGHTCLUB - NIGHT - MEMORY

A circular dance floor floats high above a futuristic virtual cityscape, its lights pulsing in neon reds and blues. It's a private party, not too crowded.

Loba, V, and Möbius members dance to a dark electronic song. Bowen glows because he's not part of the memory, just in it.

Loba is the hottest person in the room. Everyone here is sexy and beautiful, but she stands out. And it isn't just one thing. It's the way she carries herself. Mesmerizing. Hypnotic to watch her dance.

She leans close to Don's ear to be heard over the music.

LOBA

And Bowen? Tell him to come.

Don grins, drunk, eyeing her, *you like him, huh?* Loba rolls her wolf eyes, and shoves him, playfully. But she smiles, and spins away, dancing again with her unique style.

Bowen's face shifts, flattered and surprised, but he doesn't let it grow into a smile.

He gets a message from Don that reads: "Bo, I know

you're going through a lot right now, but it may be good for you to come and take your mind off it. You saw her, right? The legend wants you."

Bowen summons a floating keyboard, and as he types, the letters materialize in the smoky air.

> Thanks, buddy. I know you're trying to
> help, but I'm not in the mood. And I'm
> not interested in Loba.

He pauses, then types the harder truth.

> You know what I think about uploads.
> Have fun.

He hits ENTER and the words fade out.

INT. MÖBIUS OPS CENTER - NIGHT

The hangar is empty, dimly lit. Bowen plays pool alone. He misfires when Loba enters, wearing a cool jacket with abstract shapes and floral-like patterns.

She grimaces at the harsh *scuff*, watching the cue ball wobble a pathetic few inches.

LOBA

You know how to play?

Bowen taps the RESTART button on the rail and the balls vanish, reappearing in a perfect triangle. He grabs a pool cue from the rack and offers it to her. She reaches to grab it, but dodges it with a sly smile, choosing another cue with LOBA engraved on it.

She leans down to break, tossing her long dark curls back, her golden-yellow eyes fixed on the ball. Bowen glances at her cleavage, but quickly looks away. He is not used to seeing such beautiful women. And certainly none as unique as her.

She breaks, the pack exploding, and a striped ball sinks into the corner pocket. She circles the table like a predator.

LOBA

So where're you from?

They talk as they play on.

BOWEN

California. Have you been?

LOBA

(shaking her head)

Is it nice?

BOWEN

Yeh. I'm from a mountain town, so... you know, there's a lotta nature. A lotta beautiful hikes with views of a big blue lake. That lake is so deep it never freezes, you know? Not even in the harshest conditions. How fucking poetic is that?

LOBA

Have you been to Mount Belji?
        (he shakes his head)
It's one of the most beautiful hikes in the
United Worlds. It has a big blue lake too.
The water is –

BOWEN

        (interrupting)
Nah, sorry, it's not the same. C'mon. It's
not real nature.

LOBA

It's artificial nature.

Bowen lines up his shot, his back to her, giving her a side-eye she never sees. He doesn't want to get into that debate with her. No way.

She lowers to his level, trying to see where he's aiming.

LOBA

Mmm, you sure? You're gonna hit my
ball.

Bowen shoots anyway. The cue ball jumps, clearing hers by an inch, and *CLACK*. He sinks his shot clean. He turns over his shoulder and smiles, pressing a finger to his lips, *shhh*. Loba smiles, raising her hands in surrender.

LOBA

Alright, alright. So besides playing pool,
what do you do? For a living, I mean.

BOWEN

Now? Nothing. I used to fix robots. At a
nuclear fusion power plant.

LOBA

(stops the shot)
A nuclear fusion...? Wait.
(grins, amused)
You worked in the Offline?

BOWEN

Not only worked. I lived there. In that
small town. My whole life. 'Til now.

LOBA

Shut up. For real?

He nods and shrugs. Loba's expression softens with a
hint of nostalgia.

LOBA

Hey, no, that's cool. I grew up in a place
like that too. Well, not a mountain. A
jungle. But yeah, that was a long, long
time ago.

BOWEN

And do you miss it? When was the last
time you went to vi–

(*oops*)

...Sorry. I forgot...

LOBA

What? That I'm an upload?

He's frozen, mortified. She bumps him out of the way
with her hip, claiming space for the shot. *CLICK, CLACK.*
She sinks a ball.

Silence. Just the sound of a pool cue striking a ball,
CLICK, and balls colliding. *CLACK, CLACK, CLACK.*
CLICK. CLACK, CLACK, CLACK, CLACK.

He tries to come up with something to end the awkward
moment.

BOWEN

Nuclear fusion's amazing, don't you
think?

(off Loba's blank stare)

I mean... We went from capturing
sunlight to creating an artificial sun. How
fucking poetic is that?

Loba stops circling the table. She leans against the rail,
studying him.

LOBA

You always say that. You like poetry?

BOWEN

No, I don't know. I mean... I like when
things mean more than what they seem,
you know?

LOBA

Like our name, Möbius. You know what
it means?

He shakes his head. She steps closer, her body brushing
his, and reveals her Möbius ring without removing her
necklace. Bowen struggles to focus on the ring. Her magnetic
cleavage is right there. And her golden eyes are even more
distracting, glowing against her dark skin.

LOBA

Möbius is a loop that folds back on itself
in a way that makes you think there
are two sides, but it's just one. And you
can't tell just by looking. You have to
experience it yourself. Go ahead. Trace
it
          (grabs Bowen's finger)
with your finger. You'll see.

His finger travels through the flat Möbius-shaped ring,

and magically ends up in the same place without ever lifting his finger.

He's amazed by how cool it is. A bridge to another reality.

They lock eyes, so close they can feel each other's breath. His green eyes are honest and tormented, the kind that make you want to know all his secrets. Her golden-yellow wolf eyes are so captivating, they pull you in, and her thick, soft lips urge you to kiss and bite them all at once.

Bowen clears his throat and takes out his Möbius necklace.

> BOWEN
>
> You know, you gave me one of these before. At the music festival.
>
> (continues playing pool)
>
> It was so fuckin' cool. To see you all flying. How do you do that? Can you teach me?

> LOBA
>
> Yeah, no, it doesn't work like that. To get powers, you gotta hack the system that controls your avatar's physics. And some powers are easier to hack than others. But security always changes, so, you know, the exploit that works today won't work tomorrow.

BOWEN

And what about the guy I possessed? He had invisibility powers. Do you have that too?

LOBA

(shakes her head)

Rhea and her friends have powers nobody else has. I knew he would have cool powers 'cause he's Rhea's boyfriend.

BOWEN

Speaking of, that possession fucked me up.

(rubbing his forehead)

At one point I looked at her, at Rhea, and I felt like... I-I *liked* her. And look, I've never been in love, okay? But... Was *that* it? And I felt proud. Like we were saving the world or something, you know?

LOBA

Yeah, no, I know. Possessions are messy. Their beliefs feel right, even when they contradict your own. It's crazy, I know. It's like you inherit their truth.

> BOWEN
>
> Exactly. It's like... I get it now. Why people worship her. This guy, Warner? He really believes she saved the people. Saved them from evil corporations. And hackers. Like she's a revolutionary idol or something.

> LOBA
>
> So you're feeling empathy for them?

> BOWEN
>
> Tsk. You crazy? But, I mean, it was so fucking weird. Like... one second, she's a monster and I wanna fucking kill her. The next, she's...
>
> (shivers in disgust)
>
> I'm not gonna even say it again. But it felt like two personalities fighting inside of me, you know?

She nods, eyeing him like, *yeah, genius, I told ya, I know.* After all, she created the possession program.

> BOWEN
>
> Sorry, but I'm just thinking. What if... a piece of him... you know... stayed with me?

LOBA

You gotta question everything. Always.
You're confused right now 'cause
you were inside someone else's
consciousness. But you don't know
what other belief systems you inherited
in your life. From your friends, your
family...

He studies Loba as she sinks the last ball, growing more intrigued by the second.

LOBA

Rematch?

Chapter 8
What protects it will destroy it

14 min read

Previously...

Bowen infiltrated the Remedy lab, planted a backdoor, and killed General Zeffross. He returned to Möbius like a hero. Don took the stolen rifle to try to make replicas, but Loba warned him to clean it thoroughly. Anything Bowen brought back that wasn't originally Warner's could be traced to them.

While playing pool, Bowen asked Loba about her flying ability. She revealed powers are just hacks to the avatar's physics engine.

Bowen admitted possessing Warner had messed with his head. He felt Warner's love for Rhea, and his genuine belief that she is saving the world. Loba explained when you possess someone, you don't just control their body, but also you inherit their truths. She urged Bowen to question everything, even beliefs he could've inherited from his family.

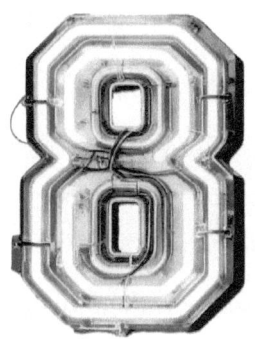

INT. MÖBIUS OPS CENTER - DAY

Loba inks a Möbius tattoo on Don's back, as a symbol of becoming a member. He checks it with a floating mirror, proud and a little in disbelief. A grin stretches the thick yellow line tattooed across his lower lip as his tongue runs over it. She signals Bowen to be next, but he shakes his head.

A ping interrupts the moment, signaling the report is ready.

At the main round table, the crew studies the final report of Rhea's weapon, the Remedy. The screens show technical information, colorful charts, and the system's architecture.

VAISHNAVI

Got 'em. All the recovery options are listed here. And look, the last backup. They made one just a few hours ago.

LOBA

They must be freaking out right now. Wipe them out, V. Wipe them all out.

V types a rapid sequence and blasts YES. A red progress bar slashes across the screen.

DELETING... 33%... 66%... 100% COMPLETE.

The screen flashes green. The crew erupts in cheers, high-fiving.

LOBA

Alright, alright. The job's not done yet. Back to your stations. We need to encrypt this.

VAISHNAVI

Hold on. Why don't we just delete it? Like we did with the backups?

J.S.

Are you kidding? We might need it.

VAISHNAVI

But someone could steal it from us. I

mean, everything is hackable. We know that better than anyone.

LOBA

Yeah, no, we get it. But J.S. has a point. We might need this to fight back. We need every edge we can get. So we're not deleting it just yet, okay? We'll be careful. Don't worry.

BOWEN
(off V's worried face)
Hey, you know what? I can build a logic bomb, so if it falls under the wrong hands, you know, we can destroy it.

Loba nods and shrugs. *Fine.* V isn't fully convinced.

* * *

A 15-foot column of translucent yellow light stands at the center of the hangar. Suspended beside it in neon text: ENCRYPTING... Hovering above the pillar: 0%.

A TIMELAPSE unfolds, turning day into night. Sunlight retreats across the hangar floor, swallowed by the electric glow of consoles and neon decorations.

No one stops. Everyone keeps working.

The light column gradually fills from the bottom up, like a vertical progress bar, a rising tide of neon yellow. The floating percentage above it updates with each surge, ending the timelapse with 97%.

Bowen shows Loba a 3D structure made of color-coded components. Behind them, Don watches, waiting for a moment to interrupt, a long heavy bag resting by his feet.

> BOWEN
> (pointing to a blue gear)
> So this component receives issues from all these other key components, right? And fixes them. It protects the entire structure. Well...

He moves his hand over a section of the structure, isolating it. Zooms in. Zooms a little bit more.

> BOWEN
> The logic bomb will unleash small tweaks here, polluting the data bit by bit. Make the Remedy unusable.

> LOBA
> So what protects it... will destroy it.

Both at the same time...

> LOBA AND BOWEN
> How fucking poetic is that?

She breaks a smile for a millisecond, containing her laughter, as she holds his gaze, amused. He smiles, embarrassed, his eyes pleading, *don't laugh at me.* And that does it. She breaks, and they burst into laughter together. She snorts, surprised she made that sound, which only makes her laugh harder. Bowen laughs harder too, clutching his stomach as she struggles to calm down.

Loba catches her breath and notices Don standing behind, watching with a smile, entertained.

> LOBA
> (to Don)
> Whatcha got there?

Don unzips the bag. It's overflowing with golden rifles.

> DON
> I reverse-engineered Zeffross' gun.

> BOWEN
> (clasping Don's hand)
> Fuck yeh, Don. Lemme see.

Bowen takes one and smiles. J.S. stands up to watch. ENCRYPTING... 99%

> LOBA
> Do they work?

> DON
> Pfft. Beauuuutifully. I shot a bunch of people and they're all dead.

Don chuckles, pleased with his own joke. Loba stares at him, her face stone, her yellow eyes boring into him until his laughter dies down.

> DON
>
> I'm just fucking with you, c'mon. You want me to shoot someone to test it? We'll know when we know. But I did thousands of replicas before. Of anything you can imagine. So... that's that.

> LOBA
>
> But never for a gun, right?

He shakes his head, lips pressed together, palms up in a silent *obviously not.*

> LOBA
>
> 'Kay. Pass 'em out. But tell 'em they might not work, okay?

As Don turns disappointed with her reaction, Rhea and dozens of United Worlds soldiers appear at the hangar doorway.

Loba smashes an EMERGENCY BUTTON, activating a red translucent protective wall in the middle of the hangar. Soldiers fire but bullets can't pass through.

Loba runs to the back wall, feeling its surface until her arm slips through. It's a hidden exit portal.

LOBA

C'mon! Hurry! Let's go!

But everyone rushes to Don, grabbing guns and lining up, ready to fight. Loba couldn't be prouder.

J.S.

(glaring at Bowen)

How the fuck did they find us?

LOBA

(to Don)

The gun. You sure you cleaned it, right?

DON

Yeah. I did. I'm sure I did.

General Akira and her troop turn their heads toward one another, surprised that Möbius has guns. Bulky, high-tech helmets with reflective blue visors hide their eyes, but their hesitation is clear. Only Akira's helmet has horns, a declaration of her rank.

Rhea stands out dressed in all black, like a widow, against the wall of blue uniforms. She looks barely out of her teens, yet she is clearly in command.

At Rhea's nudge, one soldier rushes to the protective wall and connects a device. A progress tracker materializes, floating in the air.

DEACTIVATING PROTECTION... 1%

LOBA
(whispering to herself)
Command: ghost.

Loba turns translucent like a ghost and flies straight up, passing through the ceiling without a sound.

Soldiers snap to high alert, aiming at the ceiling...

Loba ascends through the floor behind them. She recovers her normal body, able to use the golden rifle, and shoots two soldiers, clearing the way to Rhea.

IN SLOW MOTION – Dozens of soldiers turn to Loba. Aim. *BOOM*. Loba shoots Rhea first. They shoot back.

But she turns ghostly again. Bullets pass through her like air as she flies away, untouchable.

Soldiers rally around Rhea, forming a military position, covering her. She's hidden from view. The two soldiers Loba shot shake violently on the floor, screaming in pain until they die.

Loba flies through the ceiling back to the hangar,

solidifying as she lands next to Don. She gives him a small nod.

The crew erupts and goes wild. Everyone congratulates Loba for killing Rhea and taps Don on the back for reverse-engineering Zeffross' gun.

Bowen stands apart, frozen. He stares at the soldiers shielding Rhea's body. He looks like a man who has just witnessed a miracle.

Their celebrations die mid-cheer, frozen in time, when they hear a woman's light laugh cutting through the hangar.

The wall of soldiers parts. Rhea steps forward, laughing at them, her arms spread wide as if nothing happened. The gun had no effect on her.

RHEA

Loba, sweetie. You really think you can
kill me? Here? In my universe?
(scoffs)
Sweetie... I'm disappointed.

J.S. opens a box of silver discs and passes them out.

J.S.

I'm not surprised. She clearly has
security protocols no one else has. But
we'll get her out there. Use these to get
her offline location.

RHEA

(approaching the red wall)

Bowen! Hey! Bowie!

LOBA

"Bowie?" What the fuck?

J.S.

Fucking knew it! I told ya! He's a fucking
spy! A motherfuckin' spy!

J.S. throws the box and draws four golden rifles, one in
each hand, leveling them all at Bowen. Loba raises her hand
and shakes her head at J.S. She needs to hear this.

Bowen heads to the wall, stopping a few inches from
Rhea, separated only by the humming red energy. He glares
at her. Murder in his eyes.

DEACTIVATING PROTECTION... 49%

RHEA

Bowie, so nice to see you. I've been
looking for you since you were a little
kid, you know that?

BOWEN

Looking for me? What? Who the fuck do
you think I am, you dumb fuck?

RHEA
(smirks)
Bowen Huxley. 23 years old. From
Homewood, California.
(leaning closer)
Are you not?

His eyes drift to a 3D pie chart hanging on the wall in
cyberpunk style. It shows how voting power is distributed in
the United Worlds, with four slices: MYSTERY KEY holds
60% of Tores; RHEA, 20%; RHEA'S SECRET COUNCIL,
10%; THE PEOPLE, 10%.

BOWEN
You think I stole a key from you, don't
you? My neighbors told me. Your
soldiers were torturing my mom about a
key that's yours. Is the
(pointing to the pie chart)
Mystery Key what you think I got?

RHEA
(to Akira)
You were right.
(to Bowen)
Yeah, you see, Bowen... Whoever holds
that key controls the United Worlds. And
yes, you have it. Your *mom* stole it from

me and gave it to you.

BOWEN

Bullshit. I know nothing about a key.

(to Loba)

I swear, I don't know what she's talking about. My mom didn't steal shit. She was a hippie who never did any harm to anyone.

(to Rhea)

And you fucking killed her, you piece of shit. You fuckin' –

RHEA

(laughing, to Akira)

This is hilarious.

Bowen bangs his hand on the red wall, wanting to eat her alive.

BOWEN

Hey! What are you laughing at, huh?

RHEA

I'm sorry, I'm sorry. You're right. It's tragic.

(pause)

Look, I'll cut you a deal. Okay? You come with us, and I spare your friends here.

Loba steps up, shoulder-to-shoulder with Bowen.

LOBA

He's not going anywhere with you.

DEACTIVATING PROTECTION... 96%

As the device on the wall starts beeping faster, both sides scramble for cover behind workstations, tables, couches; anything they can find. The fight is on.

RHEA

Sure? 'Kay then. If that's what you want...

But remember. I tried to do the right thing.

(to her soldiers)

I'll repeat this one more time: we need him alive. Understood? Kill the others.

LOBA

(pulls Bowen violently)

Go. C'mon. Go!

Bowen shakes his head and takes out his golden gun. Loba lets it be.

DEACTIVATING PROTECTION... 99%

DEACTIVATING PROTECTION... 100%

The red translucent wall flickers and dies.

Gunfire erupts. They shoot at each other from long distances.

Loba turns ghostly and flies to unexpected places, trying to slap the tracking device on Rhea. But Rhea is too well protected, and Loba kills three soldiers in the process.

Bowen fires nonstop, wild, erratic shots in every direction. He's possessed by incendiary rage.

FROM RHEA'S POV: A blue ethereal target locks onto the workstation shielding Bowen and two others. With telekinesis, Rhea shoves the workstation aside. The target shifts to the man beside Bowen. She lifts him and smashes him against the wall. She yanks the other off his feet. Only Bowen remains.

IN SLOW MOTION – Soldiers annihilate Möbius... The front line steps over the bodies, forcing the survivors deeper into the hangar.

Rhea lifts Bowen, suspending him in the air, his body wrapped in ethereal blue energy as he fights against her invisible grip. Akira shoots him with a black paralyzer gun, and the strength drains from him in an instant as he loses all control of his body.

Rhea pulls Bowen toward her... when two Möbius fighters fly over and attack her, trying to stick the geo-tracking discs onto her. She drops Bowen and hurls the attackers aside, one after the other.

Taking advantage of this, Don and V drag Bowen toward the emergency exit portal as bullets whip past them. The three of them disappear through the portal.

J.S. types furiously at his station with his four hands, finishing the encryption on the Remedy. ENCRYPTING... 100% COMPLETE.

In the center of the hangar, the 15-foot column of yellow light fills up, and vanishes. A key materializes on J.S.' desk, and he tucks it in his pocket.

With almost no survivors left, Loba realizes they've lost. She bolts for the emergency portal. General Akira fires, but Loba disappears through the wall just in time.

INT. TEMPLE - CONTINUOUS

Loba materializes inside an ancient temple shaped like a pyramid, its stone floor covered in triangle-shaped portals glowing faintly.

Bowen lies motionless on the ground, a small device attached to his neck, pulsing rhythmically. Floating above him is a magenta status bar.

Reactivating... 27%

Don and V stand next to a floating screen that reads:

Close portal?

YES   NO

V turns to Loba.

VAISHNAVI
Who else's missing?

>   LOBA
>   Not sure. Just J.S., I think.

They hold to see if someone else arrives. Hoping.

No one comes through. V reaches for the YES button when J.S. materializes.

>   J.S.
>   Close it! Close it now!

>   LOBA
>   Wait! Are you sure?

A soldier appears and aims at Loba, but she shoots him first. J.S. smashes his fist onto the YES button.

QUICK SHOT of soldiers slamming against the hangar wall where the emergency portal was. Dozens of dead bodies cover the floor.

Beside Bowen, the magenta bar updates – Reactivating... 100% – before it vanishes.

Bowen's body unlocks. He regains control and scratches his neck, embarrassed. He notices the small device stuck and removes it from his neck.

>   BOWEN
>   Thanks... Uh, that felt so weird. I was,
>   uh, trapped in my own body. I mean, I
>   couldn't move, but you know, I could
>   feel everything. See everything.

LOBA

(to all)

Listen up, we gotta move. I'll send the
new location. 'Till then, lay low.

Everyone nods and disappears one by one through
different portals.

Artificially biological

I wore the enemy to see the show,
and felt a love I didn't want to know.
pulling the trigger with a stranger's hand,
to execute the justice I had planned.

tracing the loop along the twisted line,
to separate inherited from mine.
I question every story I was told,
and fear the lies I was raised to hold.

—Bowen Huxley

Chapter 9
Beyond nature

13 min read

Previously...

Möbius was encrypting the Remedy when Rhea and dozens of United Worlds soldiers led by General Akira ambushed their base. Rhea revealed that Bowen has the Mystery Key, which holds 60% of Tores. He denies knowing anything about it.

J.S. finished the encryption, securing the Remedy as a portable key, before escaping. Only he, Loba, Bowen, Don, and V escaped.

INT. BOWEN'S SPACE BEDROOM

Bowen collapses onto his huge bed with a beer in hand, staring through the glass ceiling at the giant ringed planet, his green, glassy eyes wide and refusing to blink.

A memory flashes FROM BOWEN'S POV (B&W): Outside his cabin at dawn, he says goodbye to his mother before leaving for the United Worlds.

> ABI (IN THE MEMORY)
> (gripping his arm)
> Don't go, Bowie. Stay. Please. I'll do better. I'll take better care of myself. No more cheese, I swear.

ABI (IN THE MEMORY)
(grabs his face)
And whatever happens, I'll be here. This
will always be your home.

The memory ends.

If only he could go back in time to the day he left her to come here. He should've stayed and taken care of her. Been with her in her last moments.

FROM BOWEN'S POV: He drifts upward through the glass ceiling toward the ringed planet. In the vast silence of space, he turns and there he is, his avatar, lying on the bed below, looking at him. His dark purple hair spreads across the pillow, purple parachute pants and dark orange boots completing the look he chose for himself. His body feels far away, like an out-of-body experience.

A memory flashes FROM BOWEN'S POV: Separated by a red translucent wall at the Möbius hideout, Bowen and Rhea face each other.

RHEA (IN THE MEMORY)
Bowie, so nice to see you. I've been looking for you since you were a little kid, you know that?

RHEA (IN THE MEMORY)
Whoever holds that key controls the United Worlds. And yes, you have it.

Your *mom* stole it from me and gave it
to you.

The memory ends.

Bowen scratches his head, struggling to understand.
He waves his hand, summoning a browser in the middle of
the room. He types "Abigail Huxley Homewood" and taps
ENTER.

0 RESULTS FOUND

Bowen frowns. He tries again. "Abigail Huxley."

0 RESULTS FOUND

Frustrated, he grabs a picture of his mother from the
photo wall. He throws it into the browser, letting the system
scan her face.

NO MATCHES FOUND. IDENTITY
UNKNOWN.

Impossible. Everyone has at least one record. It's as if
she never existed.

INT. CINEMA

Sitting on the edge of a comfy couch facing a massive
screen, Bowen can't take his eyes off the REPRESSED
memories folder, biting his nails. He sips his beer, scratching
his head, dread crawling in. What will he find there?

Finally summoning the courage, he takes a deep breath,

chugs his beer, and points a finger at the screen. The REPRESSED folder responds with a glowing white aura to show it is selected. He taps the empty air and the folder ripples like water. A warning message pops up.

> Repressed memories are a defense
> mechanism. The content might be
> disturbing.
>
> $499 to access.
>
> OPEN   CLOSE

He drinks. Drinks again, the beer bottle clenched tight in his hand. With a quick, whip-like tap, as if already regretting the decision, he hits OPEN.

Inside the folder, the repressed memories appear organized chronologically. Glowing bubbles marked with numbers show how many memories exist at each age, and they're all from his first five years of life.

Bowen scratches his head again, harder this time, nervous, unsure if he should keep going. He chugs his beer, afraid of what he'll find, and expands the bubbles big enough to see clips inside them, showing shaky fragments from a shady underground lab.

In one of those clips, strapped to an operating table, 5-year-old Bowen cries his soul out as a scientist performs experiments on him. He's too little to be suffering so much.

Another clip shows little Bowen crouched in the shadows

of a dark lab, knees pulled tight to his chest. He is shaking and crying silently, trying to make himself small, trying to disappear.

Bowen is trembling now. He should stop. He needs to stop. But he spots the final clip, the very last memory in the dark lab. He aims at it, and as he taps the empty air, he finds himself in...

INT. UNDERGROUND LAB - NIGHT - MEMORY

Bodies of men, women, and children float in red gel inside tall cylindrical bioreactors. Neither dead nor alive.

In the center of the room, an old BIOENGINEER in a red lab coat shaves 5-year-old Bowen's head. His sharp red cheekbones stand out against his pale, skeletal face, and glowing around his collar is a bioluminescent tattoo that reads CODER OF LIFE.

Little Bowen sits on a stool, trembling. A dark stain spreads across his pants. He pees himself in terror.

> BIOENGINEER
> Hey, don't be scared, kid. I won't let anything hurt you. You're very special, you know that? Nature couldn't have made you on its own. You're the smartest kid we've ever **engineered**.
> (smiles proudly)
> You're beyond nature.

The bioengineer chugs from a silver flask engraved with the Golden Gate Bridge, watching the kid from the corner of his eye, expecting gratitude or excitement. But the kid just shakes, silent and terrified, a tear rolling down his cheek.

Annoyed, the bioengineer grabs him, strapping him face-down on the operating table. He fits a mask over his nose and mouth before turning the gas valve. Little Bowen doesn't even try to break free, too familiar with the experiments.

FROM 5-YEAR-OLD BOWEN'S POV: The hiss of gas fills his ears. Through the tears, all he can see are the cracked white tiles of the floor, blurred by the water in his eyes. His eyelids flutter, heavy, fighting gravity, before finally falling shut. Darkness.

INT. CINEMA

Bowen sits by the edge of the couch, fighting to breathe, his hands shaking.

> BIOENGINEER (V.O.)
> You're the smartest kid we've ever **engineered**.

Bowen squeezes his eyes shut.

> BIOENGINEER (V.O.)
> ...smartest kid we've ever **engineered**.

BIOENGINEER (V.O.)

...engineered... engineered...

Bowen stands up and grabs his head, dropping the beer.

BIOENGINEER (V.O.)

(proudly)

You're beyond nature.

A cheerful chime cuts through the panic. A magenta pop-up materializes in midair.

Get therapy now! ~~$79~~ $49/hour.

He grabs the glowing ad with both hands and throws it against the wall, where it shatters into pieces that fade away.

INT. BOWEN'S SPACE STATION

He drinks at his private bar, a wide oval window in front of him framing the alien planet, glowing alone in the dark. His eyes shine with tears as he stares at a selfie of him and his mother. She was already sick when the picture was taken, and it had started to show, especially around the eyes, puffy and swollen, and the pale skin. But her smile is big and grateful, holding on to a sunny day at the lake with her son.

He slams a shot of blue liquor and pours another.

A memory flashes FROM BOWEN'S POV: Rhea lifts Bowen, suspending him in the air, his body wrapped in ethereal blue energy as he struggles to break free from her telekinesis.

The memory ends.

His face hardens, a deep furrow cutting through it as rage twitches beneath the skin. He downs the drink.

* * *

Bowen glows in the center of a dark glass sphere dome, surrounded by screens. He hacks and listens to electronic music.

A log entry catches his attention, glowing in red.

> DEBUG: JNDI Lookup failed on remote
> resource request.

BOWEN
Command: what's this logging system?
Tell me everything a security engineer
should know about LogVR.

He scrolls through the documentation, reading and learning. A thread with comments written by the program's creator saying, "Sorry for the delays. This was supposed to be a passion project!" "Need more maintainers, it's just me." "Overwhelmed here... Help."

As he digs through the code, he finds something exciting. He leans closer, tilts his head, and a small smile tugs at the corner of his mouth.

He types with one hand, drinking beer with the other, absorbed by the screens. He taps ENTER.

ACCESS GRANTED

He chokes on his beer. He coughs, wiping his mouth, staring at the screen. *It actually worked.*

He opens a file and his avatar's blueprint materializes around him. It's an immersive, gigantic 3D map of interconnected color-coded nodes resembling a neural network.

Startled, he stands up, staggering back. He is standing inside his own source code.

He enlarges a node called "Avatar Movement Component," with settings for WALK, SWIM, and FLIGHT. He swipes WALK and SWIM to max speeds, but FLIGHT is grayed out. No way to enable it.

He pushes deeper into the nodes, finding one labeled "Physics Constraint Actor." His eyes widen in surprise. The switches for TELEKINESIS and FLIGHT are marked LOCKED and flash in red. He flips them to FREE, and the lights turn green.

He looks up through the glass dome at the ringed planet above. A smile breaks across his face.

EXT. BOWEN'S SPACE STATION

Bowen flies around the curve of his massive white Space Station, exhilarated. A week ago, this was a fantasy. Now, it's a dream come true.

He lets out a wild shout, half laughter, half disbelief, as

he swoops close to the wide ring. The structure spins slowly around a spine-like central hub, its smooth surface dotted with blinking lights and antennas, glittering like stars pinned to its skin.

INT. BOWEN'S SPACE STATION

He flies back inside, out of control. As he lands, he slams into the ground, skidding awkwardly before tumbling onto his back.

Something slips from his jacket pocket and skids across the floor. His big smile vanishes. It's a syringe filled with yellow liquid.

A memory flashes FROM WARNER'S POV: At the lab, Bowen is possessing Warner when General Zeffross enters. Warner hides below the desk.

> ZEFFROSS (IN THE MEMORY)
> I saw you! What're you doing?

Warner reappears behind the desk. With a sleight of hand, he slips the syringe with yellow liquid into his side pocket.

> WARNER (IN THE MEMORY)
> Sorry, I hid 'cause... You know... Doc said
> nobody should see me here. Why are
> you here?

The memory ends.

He picks up the syringe.

A memory flashes FROM WARNER'S POV: After killing General Zeffross, Bowen admires the powerful rifle.

> WARNER (IN THE MEMORY)
> Will the gun come with me?

> LOBA (IN THE MEMORY)
> Yes. Anything you hold that wasn't Warner's will get transported too.

Another memory flashes FROM BOWEN'S POV: At the Möbius hideout, Loba points at the golden rifle in Don's hands.

> LOBA (IN THE MEMORY)
> (to Don)
> Hey, you need to clean that, okay? It's very important. They can trace it back to us 'cause it wasn't Warner's.

The memory ends.

Bowen's green eyes open wide, wild, realizing it was his fault. It was his fault the U.W. Army found the Möbius base. He didn't clean the syringe like Don did with the gun. And now they're all dead because of him.

He reaches over his shoulder, clawing at his own back, gripping his shoulders tight, like he's trying to hold himself in. He's cursed. He is fucking cursed.

* * *

Bowen lies super drunk on the floor beneath his private bar. An empty bottle rolls across the floor, the hollow sound echoing in the silence.

He has his black hood up, framing a face pale with exhaustion. He gazes at the glowing syringe with glassy green eyes. Intoxicated by hopelessness, he wonders whether this life is worth living.

Slowly, he presses the needle against the soft skin of his forearm. His thumb hovers over the plunger, trembling. One push. Just one. That is all it takes to make the noise stop.

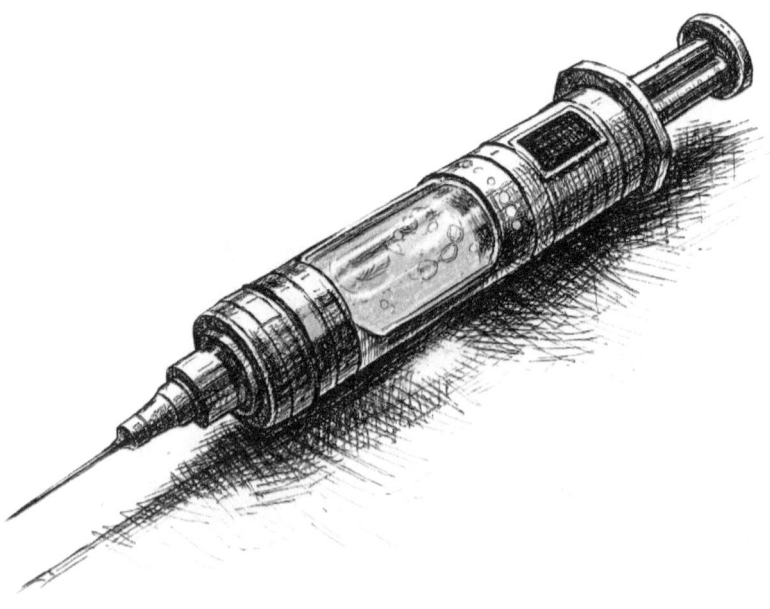

He exhales, his finger tightening.

PING.

A magenta notification from the Memory app appears in midair.

> Do you wish to relieve happy
> memories?

He drops the syringe and hurls the empty bottle across the space station. He hates how they can read his mind. It's so fucking creepy.

He stares at the Möbius necklace, biting his lip. As long as he wears it, Rhea can't spy on his feelings and memories. His violent breath calms down.

EXT. FOREST - AFTERNOON - MEMORY

FROM BOWEN'S POV: His mother, Abi, is right there. Alive. She is in her 40s, healthy and vibrant, her skin glistening with sweat. It's a hot summer day.

They hike up a steep mountain trail, cutting through the woods, dodging the sunlight that leaks through the canopy.

IN SLOW MOTION – A family of majestic deer appears out of nowhere, thundering past them, inches away, shaking the ground with powerful strides and resonant sounds.

Bowen and Abi look at each other, their mouths open, their eyes saying, *did that really just happen?*

The memory freezes. The deer stop in midair. An ad

materializes with Rhea promoting Secret Vaults:

RHEA (ON VIDEO)

Passwords can be cracked. Faces can be
faked. But thieves can't fake your mind.
That's why I trust Secret Vaults.

A memory flashes FROM WARNER'S POV: Inside a vault,
he massages Rhea's shoulders as she sits before a floating
screen, using all her Tores to vote on new laws.

The memory ends.

RHEA (ON VIDEO)

It scans your brain to authenticate you,
making Secret Vaults unhackable. The
most secure storage system in the Uni–

The ad continues but the sound fades, muffled. Bowen
stares, thinking... struggling with his drunkenness.

BOWEN

Command: Secret Vaults uses LogVR?

He waits, wincing, already bracing for disappointment.

Chapter 10
Human Preservation Act

8 min read

Previously...

Bowen hacked his avatar's physics, unlocking Flight and Telekinesis. But the victory shattered when he discovered a stolen yellow syringe in his pocket, the tracker that led the Army to Möbius.

Realizing the massacre was his fault, Bowen nearly ended his life, until an ad for Rhea's Secret Vaults sparked an idea. If her unhackable vaults run on the same vulnerable code he just cracked, he might have found a way in.

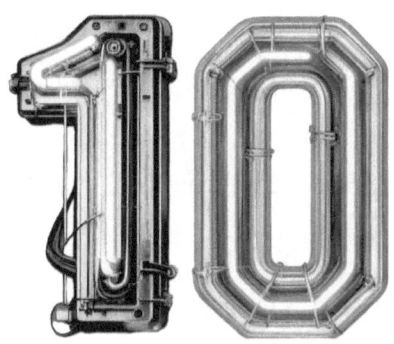

INT. MÖBIUS OPS CENTER - DAY

The new Möbius hideout is another massive repurposed airplane hangar, identical to the last one but hidden in a different corner of the Worlds. It feels much bigger and emptier now that so few survived the devastating ambush.

Loba, V, and Don stand before the Memorial Wall, where the fallen are reanimated as 3D statues. Dozens of familiar faces have been added, staring back at them.

VAISHNAVI

(hugging Loba)

Any news from J.S.?

Loba shakes her head, and V doesn't hide her concern,

suspecting J.S. might be onto something.

A whooshing sound at the hangar doorway makes everyone turn and pull out their golden rifles.

> DON
> (lowering his weapon)
> Fuck, Bo. Where were you?

> BOWEN
> ...I'm sorry. I'm really... sorry.
> (takes out the syringe)
> How could I forget? I took it. When I was inside Warner. That's how they tracked us down. It's my fault.

> LOBA
> And you brought it back here?!

> BOWEN
> It's clean now.

> LOBA
> You have to be fucking kidding me.
> (pointing to the wall)
> Look what you did. All dead because of you.

> BOWEN
> You think I don't know? I'm sorry.

LOBA

You should go. Get outta here.

Bowen is hurt, but he doesn't argue. He gets it. He'll have to live with this guilt all his life, just like his mother's horrible death. He turns and walks away, defeated.

DON

Bo! Wait.

(to Loba)

Hey, c'mon. He was in shock, Loba. You really think he meant to lead them here? I mean, General Zeffross was about to kill him. I'd forget I had the syringe too if I were him.

VAISHNAVI

And, you know, he killed Zeffross.

Loba glares at her, but V stands her ground.

VAISHNAVI

(pointing to Loba's rifle)

He took Zeffross' gun, and now, we can fight back. He even planted a backdoor in the Remedy. If it weren't for him, Rhea would still have the power to use that fucked-up tech and turn everyone in the United Worlds into her slaves.

(pause)

He earned his place.

V fixes Loba with a look that says, *and you know it.* Loba touches her wolf ears, then exhales and rolls her golden-yellow eyes. She knows they're right.

Bowen walks back to the group. Don clasps his hand and pulls him into a hug.

DON

Hey, you okay?

Bowen lifts his eyebrows and tilts his head. *No, but what are you going to do?*

DON

What about the key? You know, the Mystery Key. You don't have it, right?

BOWEN

I swear. I know nothing about it.

(pause)

But I know how to end her.

(pause)

I'm gonna hack into Rhea's secret vault and steal her Tores.

LOBA

(ironically)

Oh yeah? You're gonna hack into Rhea's

vault? That's brilliant. Don't know why we didn't think of doing that before. Right, V?

BOWEN

Look... You know LogVR, right? You probably know it. It's the universal logging framework for VR technology. Very, very old. Used everywhere. And like most open source, only one person maintains it. Not very secure.
(leans in)
Well... I found a flaw in that system. And you know what program also uses LogVR? Secret Vaults.

Everyone is taken aback. He might be onto something.

BOWEN

You know, the portal to get inside the vault scans your brain and sends your brain map to the Brain Bank. Their system checks to see if it's a match to the authorized person, which in this case would be Rhea.

VAISHNAVI

And when they scan ours, it will say "no

match."

BOWEN

Right! But when the Brain Bank sends the "no match" response to the portal, we can exploit this flaw in LogVR to trick the vault into thinking it's a match.

LOBA

But even if it works, and I want to see the code before I believe a word of it, you're forgetting something. We have no idea where the fucking portal is to get inside the vault. You can't hack it from here. You know that, right?

BOWEN

Yes, I know, Loba. But hear me out. When I possessed Warner, I got these flashbacks, these memories, of walking inside the painting. I don't know if you remember it. That huge painting of a road cutting through poppy fields?

A memory flashes FROM WARNER'S POV: Rhea and Warner are inside that painting, kissing passionately in the poppy fields.

The memory ends.

BOWEN

And then I was inside a vault with Rhea.

And she was using her Tores.

(pause)

I-I think the portal is inside that painting.

They exchange glances, unsure.

DON

Fuck it.

(clasps Bowen's hand)

I'm with ya, man.

(to Loba and V)

C'mon. It's worth a shot, right?

Loba stands with her hands crossed, body turned away like she doesn't want to hear Bowen.

VAISHNAVI

...I guess. You know what? Every year, she throws this big party to celebrate Founding Day. All the famous people go. We can use this flaw to possess one of them and get in.

BOWEN

Yeh, no, we can't. This exploit works by sending a payload to a vulnerable server, not directly to a personal device.

It doesn't give us control over a person.

VAISHNAVI

Okay... So possessing someone takes a fuck load of research, several weeks, and that party is in what? Two days? We'll need to –

A beeping sound interrupts V. A floating screen materializes with an urgent broadcast, its lower third reading, "EMERGENCY ADDRESS ON NATIONAL SECURITY."

Rhea stands behind a podium, its wooden surface carved with the U.W. insignia. She is dressed in all black, like a widow, making her freckles and green eyes pop. Beside her stands General Akira and high-ranking officers, their faces hidden behind reflective blue visors. Behind them, the United Worlds flag hangs, its dark blue and black stripes running vertically.

RHEA (ON VIDEO)

My fellow citizens. Last night, our nation was shaken by a cowardly attack. The terrorist group Möbius murdered General Zeffross and 13 brave soldiers.

(pause)

Our forces fought back and dismantled nearly their entire organization. Only five of them are still out there, including their soulless leader, Loba,

          (with heavy disdain)

an *upload*.

MOST WANTED posters burst from the screen and hover in the air beneath it, showcasing Loba, Bowen, Don, V, and J.S.

          RHEA (ON VIDEO)

Let me be clear. Your safety is my highest priority. That is why

          (pointing to Akira)

General Akira Sakai, one of our strongest leaders, has returned from retirement to lead us through this crisis.

Rhea goes around the podium, moving closer. It feels intimate but commanding.

          RHEA (ON VIDEO)

Now, we must speak honestly about uploads. The United Worlds has 99 million uploads. And each and every one of them is the cause and beneficiary of our nation's crisis.

          (pause)

Too many hardworking men and women are losing their jobs to uploads. Why? Because uploads accept lower wages. Wages no citizen could survive on. They don't have to pay for lifepods like we do. They don't need healthcare like we do.

(pause)

But this isn't just about jobs. It's about something more. Something deeper.

(pause)

It's about the very soul of our nation. Uploads look like us. Talk like us. But they're just code. They're not really alive. They're not human.

(pause)

An upload can say it loves you. But only a soul can mean it.

(pause)

Uploads are the great masters of deception. Far more dangerous than we realize. They are destabilizing our economy. They are destabilizing our communities. And they are destabilizing our humanity itself.

(pause)

So we must act now, before it's too late. We cannot let them decide the fate of the human race. It's our duty. That's why I'm introducing the Human Preservation Act. This legislation determines the following.

(pause)

Two weeks after the vote results are published, if the Human Preservation Act passes by the will of the majority... all uploads will be deleted.

DON

Deleted? She said deleted?

From behind, V puts her hand on Loba's shoulder. Loba steps forward, closer to the broadcast, her eyes locked on Rhea, not wanting to miss anything she says. The air is tense. Heavy. It's a moment that will be remembered in history.

RHEA (ON VIDEO)

Look, I do not bring this forward lightly. But it's necessary to protect the human race. To protect our future. The future of our children.

(pause)

So now, I ask you, fellow citizens. Stand with me. Vote for the Human Preservation Act. And together, we will rebuild and strengthen our nation. You have that power.

(pause)

Thank you.

The broadcast ends and the screen vanishes. The MOST WANTED posters drift down slowly, swaying from side to side until they touch the ground.

They all look at Loba, who's infuriated. Somehow, her golden-yellow wolf eyes glow more intensely.

LOBA
(to Bowen)
Your plan better work.

Chapter 11
Am I tech?

23 min read

Previously...

Bowen revealed a plan to steal Rhea's Tores by hacking her Secret Vault, which is hidden inside a massive painting at her secret chamber.

Every year, Rhea hosts a party at her castle to celebrate Founder Day. Möbius has two days to possess one of the guests and infiltrate the gala.

The stakes exploded when Rhea broadcasted a national address, introducing the Human Preservation Act, a law that would delete all uploads.

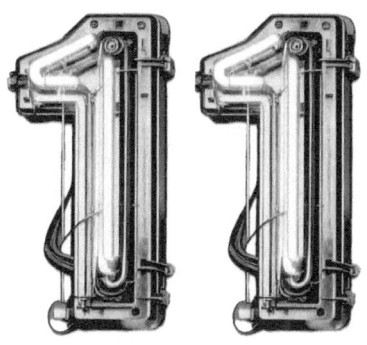

INT. MÖBIUS OPS CENTER - NIGHT

Loba, Bowen, V, and Don work on their stations, tired and frustrated. All day trying to possess someone, and nothing. Loba slams the desk and stomps off, touching her wolf ears.

> LOBA
> Fuck. We'll have to go with plan B.

> VAISHNAVI
> No, wait. You sure?

> LOBA
> I know it's riskier, but we don't have enough time for a possession.

She taps PRINT and a potion bottle with transparent liquid materializes on her desk.

> BOWEN
> (pointing at the potion)
> Your program is in there?

Loba nods. They smile, finding it very cool, as always with her.

> LOBA
> You know, tickets, like for Rhea's party, are stored in external endpoints inside people's wallets. Makes it easier for security to validate them fast.
> (lifting the potion)
> Well, my program extracts all the tickets from a wallet. We just need the victim to drink it.

> VAISHNAVI
> Julius Rasek is at Earthrise.

> BOWEN
> What? Who is where?

> DON
> Julius Rasek. Very famous.

VAISHNAVI
He posted a memory just now. He's at
Earthrise nightclub.

LOBA
He's going to Rhea's party?

VAISHNAVI
He goes every year.

LOBA
(to Bowen and Don)
You boys are gonna need new avatars.

* * *

They stand near the exit portal. As they tap ACTIVATE on their wrists, they transform into new avatars. V becomes an Indian fashion model with oversized sunglasses. Don expands, growing a foot taller, turning into a red alien. A colorful, scaled frill fans out around his neck, like a venomous prehistoric lizard, and his eyes narrow into cold, yellow reptilian slits.

Loba shifts into a gothic icon, with a horn-shaped headdress covering her wolf ears, and a sheer black lace veil draping across her golden eyes. Her thick, soft lips are painted with black lipstick. Her body is wrapped in a see-through black dress that reveals dark red lingerie underneath.

Bowen morphs into a handsome humanoid robot, but keeps his unmistakable green eyes. He is dressed like a pastor, in a long purple robe with a prominent white cross on his chest. He removes the wide-brimmed black hat with a nod, revealing a human brain beneath a transparent dome.

They step onto the exit portal and – *whoosh* – disappear.

EXT. EARTHRISE NIGHTCLUB - NIGHT

They materialize in their new avatars at an outdoor nightclub on the surface of the Moon, where an exaggerated huge Earth rises from the darkness of space.

At the entrance, two opposing groups hand out pamphlets. One group, waves signs that read, UPLOADS LIVE. UPLOADS LOVE. UPLOADS FEEL. UPLOADS RIGHTS ARE HUMAN RIGHTS. Their pamphlets mimic the decagon badge all uploads are forced to wear on their shoulders. Bowen gets one and reads it.

UPLOADS LIVE

DON'T BE COMPLICIT IN THE
BIGGEST GENOCIDE IN HISTORY

VOTE NO ON THE HUMAN PRESERVATION ACT

Across from them, the opposing group wears shirts with Rhea's face stylized like a revolutionary icon. Bowen takes one of the pamphlets they're distributing.

STOP THE UPLOADS

PROTECT OUR JOBS
PROTECT OUR FAMILIES
SAVE HUMANITY

VOTE YES FOR HUMAN PRESERVATION ACT

Beneath the STOP THE UPLOADS headline, Loba's face appears inside a crossed-out circle, like a political enemy poster.

Bowen shows it to Loba and the crew, who exchange worried glances, a reminder of what is at stake. As if they needed one.

The ANTI-UPLOAD ACTIVIST who handed out the flyer leans in close to Bowen, pointing at the pro-upload protesters.

>   ANTI-UPLOAD ACTIVIST
>   They say genocide?
>   (laughs)
>   You can't kill what's already dead, right?

Bowen forces a smile. The activist stares at them as they enter, his eyes narrowing suspiciously.

They push toward the back, following V through the thumping bass. A deep house song pulses through the nightclub, eerie and ancient, like an alien ritual carried by drums and a woman's mystical voice.

In the VIP section, raised on a platform above the dance floor, celebrity JULIUS RASEK dances with his hot friends around a table covered with champagne bottles. Everyone loves him and wants to be in his orbit.

> VAISHNAVI
> (pointing to Rasek)
> That's the guy.

They climb the stairs, and as they walk into the VIP, their avatars flash red. An invisible force moves them back outside. Three young women, so skinny they'd be considered anorexic in the Offline, flash green as they get in.

> BOWEN
> Give it to me.

Bowen grabs the potion out of Loba's hand and opens the cap.

> BOWEN
> Command: telek.

A blue ethereal target locks onto the potion.

DON

No fucking way. Get outta here!

Loba and V exchange a look, surprised he hacked that power, one they had considered impossible to crack.

Bowen floats the potion over, very high so people don't see it, and tips it into Rasek's drink, without anyone noticing, except one who shakes his head and rubs his eyes, believing he is too drunk.

The crew stares, anxious, waiting for Rasek to take a sip. Rasek laughs at a joke, raises his glass, and chugs it.

Loba huddles the group. They lean in toward her as light spills from her wrist, forming a floating screen with a loading bar spinning...

The screen lights up green, revealing two tickets to Rhea's party. They look at each other realizing it's on.

LOBA

(to Bowen)

Looks like you're coming with me tomorrow.

(to all)

'Kay Möbius, this could be our last night alive. Let's make it count.

The beat drops. Loba throws her head back and howls like a wolf on the hunt, a long, wild *AWOOOOO* that blends perfectly with the music.

* * *

Earth has risen from darkness. It's twenty times larger than the real planet Earth.

The four of them dance to a sexy, violent sequence of a techno house track. Bowen and Loba move in sync, their bodies brush against each other, connected. Strong sexual tension. It's far more than just a dance. Somehow, their new avatars make it feel even more special, like it's not about their bodies, but it's about their souls. It's spiritual but sexy at the same time.

V grabs Bowen's robe, pulling him closer, and gives him a sly smile. But he barely notices, his eyes locked on Loba, completely consumed by her.

Don drinks and drinks and drinks, wasted, stumbling into strangers.

An alarm cuts through the music, which stops dead. Thousands of dancers turn toward Earth, cheering, waiting, holding their breath for the show they know is coming.

Out of the darkness of space, a blazing streak of light tears through the void toward the blue planet, growing larger by the second until it becomes a blinding fireball.

The planet-killer meteor crashes against Earth and destroys it in slow-motion, fire and lava bursting across continents.

The music kicks back in, louder than before. They dance

as the world burns, fragments of Earth drifting above them.

VAISHNAVI
(shouting over the noise)
I THINK I'LL GO HOME.

Bowen and Loba don't register anything around them, locked together, smiling, challenging each other with their eyes.

LOBA
(to Bowen's ear)
Let's go to my place.

Don puts one arm around Loba and another around Bowen, swaying like a gigantic red pendulum. Bowen bursts into laughter.

BOWEN
We're moving it to Loba's.

Don raises his glass and nods, signaling he's in. Loba forces a smile, then exhales through her nose. She leans over and whispers something into V's ear.

EXT. LOBA'S JUNGLE - NIGHT

A series of magnificent waterfalls cascade over cliffs.

Not far away to the right, a stylish bamboo house sits high in the tallest tree of a lush jungle.

Howler monkeys roar, cicadas buzz, frogs croak. The

jungle feels alive.

INT. LOBA'S LIVING ROOM - CONTINUOUS

Back in their usual avatars, they lie on a bohemian rug, their heads touching at the center forming a circle, sharing a fat joint, listening to a mellow acoustic guitar song that is peaceful.

BOWEN

(long smoke, keeps it in)

I like how it burns my throat.

(exhales with a smile, touching

the soft rug)

Your place is so cool.

Round windows of different sizes cover the bamboo walls, and two f-shaped skylights in the high ceiling let moonlight in.

LOBA

It's from a weird dream I had.

V sits on a bohemian cushion next to a low center table covered with music sheets and pencils. She makes room for a greasy cheeseburger that materializes on a plate, then gobbles it.

VAISHNAVI

(mouth full)

I'd be so fat in the Offline.

(pointing to the exotic plant with
red flowers)

Mm. Love that plant. What is it?

LOBA

That one? I made it. It grows with
moonlight, not sunlight.

As Don stands up, he loses balance and spills his drink
onto one of the bohemian cushions scattered around,
annoying Loba. He steadies himself against the classic grand
piano, trying to fight the dizziness.

BOWEN

Don, you okay?

Don lifts his thumb and shambles toward the back
hallway.

LOBA

Hey! Where are you going?

(pointing to the opposite way)

Exit is that way.

Don ignores her, disappearing into one of the rooms.
Bowen just laughs and shakes his head. Loba smiles and
frowns. *What is he doing?*

VAISHNAVI

(finishing the burger)

Okay. This was delish. I'm much better now.

    (standing)

Going to bed.

LOBA

Night, V.

BOWEN

Bye, V.

VAISHNAVI

    (warning tone)

Big day ahead.

She gives them a knowing look. Bowen and Loba lock eyes, smiling. V waves as she disappears through the portal.

Outside Loba's treehouse, torrents of rain pour over the dense canopy. Lightning blinks through the lush vegetation, followed by the rumbles of thunder.

Lying close to each other on the colorful bohemian rug, Loba and Bowen appreciate the storm's symphony, her curls fan out in a thick black halo.

BOWEN

Don't you love the sound of rain?

LOBA

Why do you think it's raining?

He chuckles, realizing she configured the rain.

                    LOBA
          Nature's music.

                    BOWEN
          So how long have you played piano?

                    LOBA
          Since before I can remember. My dad
          taught me. I was barely walking when I
          started learning. I always wanted to be a
          musician.

                    BOWEN
          And what happened?

She gives him a *what do you think?* look, and rolls her
golden-yellow eyes, smiling. Their hands almost touch.

                    LOBA
          You? What'd you wanna be?

                    BOWEN
          I've always liked building old stuff, you
          know? Robots, machines... Love that.
          Using tech that doesn't exist anymore.
          It's kinda romantic, don't you think?

                    LOBA
          You're a tech nostalgic?

BOWEN

Kinda. I like very, very old stuff. I'm talking about tech that disappeared before my time.

LOBA

So you're nostalgic for a time you've never lived.

BOWEN
(laughs)

Yeh, I guess so. Not much of a career in that space, as you can imagine. Nobody wants to buy old stuff. People forget how magical technology is. Get used to it. They get so used to it that, even back home where everyone hates tech with all their heart, they use electricity every day.
(off her confused face)

Don't you see what I'm saying? Electricity was cutting-edge tech in the 19th century. Changed everything. But now? Nobody sees it as tech. If we were living in those times, I'm pretty sure my town would've condemned lightbulbs.

LOBA

(laughing)

I'm gonna take a wild guess and say you didn't have a lotta friends.

BOWEN

Everyone hated me for liking those things. Probably would've been better off as a thief or a drug addict, you know what I mean?

They laugh together. He catches her looking at his crooked teeth, so he presses his lips together.

LOBA

Hey. No. Don't. I like it. Everyone here has the same perfect teeth. Yours... has personality.

He shoots her a playful *fuck off* look, then smiles, a bit embarrassed.

BOWEN

Okay, so. I gotta admit. I always loved old tech, but virtual reality? The United Worlds? Ugh. To me, it was a place where people went to avoid reality. A deadly sin. It represented everything that's wrong with humanity. I couldn't understand

how people could waste their lives in
something that's not real. Like people
choosing consciously, without anyone
forcing them, *choosing* to give up their
freedom to live in a coffin.

LOBA

A coffin?

BOWEN

A lifepod. That's what we used to call 'em
back home. But, you know, when you're
here, you get it. And to tell you the truth,
I've never felt more alive. I mean, I can
see colors here.

LOBA
(laughing)
Oh, shut up. That's so corny!
(off Bowen's confused face)
That metaphor. "I see colors." C'mon.

BOWEN
What? No. It's not a metaphor.
(laughs)
I have this condition where I can't see
colors. At least not in the Offline. But
here I can. You don't know how magical it

was to see it for the first time. Everything was vibrant. Saturated. Felt like I was on another planet. And seeing myself in color? Seeing my mom? I can't...

LOBA

Yeah, I know. This place can be special. Offline? I couldn't walk.

BOWEN

Fuck. Really? And here you fly!

(they laugh)

This place... This place isn't where people come to avoid reality. This is reality. Just a bit different. But it's as real as the physical world, you know what I mean?

LOBA

I mean... I'm an upload. For me it's even more real than the physical world.

They laugh. His eyes rest on her dark smooth thighs beneath her tight golden shorts.

BOWEN

You know... And don't get mad, I don't think this anymore, okay? But.

(thinks how to say it)

I, uh... I used to believe uploads weren't...
real people.

LOBA

Oh, a purist, huh?

He presses his lips together and winces, ashamed he once thought that way.

BOWEN

And it's funny 'cause I was –

He cuts himself off, realizing he was sharing too much.

LOBA

(playfully hitting him, laughing)
What? C'mon. Tell me. Tell me!

He gazes at her honest wolf eyes for a few seconds, finding it cute how her wolf ears move, eager to listen.

BOWEN

Fine. Fuck. I don't even know how to say
this. I just found out, actually. But... The
other day, uh, I relived some repressed
memories. Trying to figure out why Rhea
thinks I have her key.
(sighs)
Well, uh... I... I. Wasn't. ...Born.

He shakes his head, hearing how weird it sounds.

BOWEN

I-I was bioengineered. Grown in a
fucking lab somewhere. Who knows?

She looks away, stunned. She didn't see that coming.

He scratches his head, his eyes dart left to right, searching
for words. How do you explain the feeling of being built?

BOWEN

Yeh, it was fucking traumatizing. I
mean, the clips I saw, the memories,
were fucking terrifying. No wonder I've
repressed all that. It was fucking torture.

(pause)

And I'm pretty sure my mom is not my
biological mother. No way she'd allow
the shit they did to me. No fucking way.
You don't know how sweet she is. Was.

(grimaces, swallows hard)

I actually think she worked there. At the
lab. And she rescued me.

(pause)

And you know what? Now that I know,
I have this feeling... that I really always
knew. Like I've always felt she had saved
me from something. It's weird. I know.

(pause)

And now that I think about it, I may not even have biological parents. I mean, maybe they used DNA from 100 people to create me. Who knows? So I've got, what? Like 100 moms and dads?

A nervous laugh escapes his lips. She gives him a supportive smile.

BOWEN

And why the fuck did they build me? Right? Why am I here?

(pause)

And here's the thing... So I was telling you, right? I grew up in this religious community where everyone hates tech. And I always felt like, you know, a sinner for liking machines. Like I was going to hell, for sure. And now... what? Am I... tech?

(laughs)

I'm biological *and* artificial at the same time. If that makes sense.

LOBA

Artificially biological. How fucking poetic is that?

They burst into laughter. She snorts and covers her

nose and mouth, embarrassed, but she continues snorting and laughing. She feels so ridiculous, she laughs harder, making him laugh harder. They're crying, not about her joke anymore, but at the situation. It was definitely a good joint.

Once they're able to calm down a bit, they lock eyes, wiping tears of laughter. Her understanding gaze is special. A special energy flows between them. Their eyes shut, enjoying the music, the storm... each other.

Her knees rest on his waist. As he feels her smooth thighs, she trails her fingers up his arm, leaving goosebumps. His hand grazes the edge of her perfect breasts, careful not to touch them. She breathes heavily into his ear. His fingertips trail downward, slowly, and run along her waistline, causing her to involuntarily tighten her belly. More goosebumps. She bites her thick lip, trying to resist the exploding urge to kiss him, then licks her sexy soft lips, leaving them wet and glistening.

Finally, she exhales, having held her breath longer than normal, and faces him, still with her eyes shut, asking him to kiss her. As he opens his eyes, he moves his lips inches away from hers, feeling each other's warm, accelerated breath. She leans to kiss him but he moves away, teasing. She smiles.

He doesn't make her wait any longer. He leans back in, capturing her lips in a deep, passionate kiss.

They lift off the rug, floating in the room like there is no gravity, pressing hard against each other, fusing into a ball of love energy. The light bursts in all directions, expanding until it floods everything.

EXT. LOBA'S JUNGLE - DAWN

Sunlight breaks through the clouds in a green-yellow sky, casting a golden glow over the mist and thriving foliage.

A single purple passion flower blooms in the mist. It is just one of hundreds, a violet sea carpeting the jungle floor amidst bright fern and moss.

Black ants walk in a line across the dirt, stepping over a snake's molted skin.

High in the canopy, silhouettes of howler monkeys feast on the leaves.

A green frog jumps from a mossy bank into a rushing river, sending ripples toward a yellow heliconia flower. The current catches in, sweeping its unnatural shape downstream. A powerful roar builds, as the flower plunges into a massive waterfall.

Two miles of waterfalls cascade down 300-foot cliffs, thundering into the basin below.

INT. LOBA'S BEDROOM - CONTINUOUS

They lie naked and tangled in the sheets of a large bed, drinking water, catching their breath.

The minimalist room has a grand piano next to a curved glass wall that frames the artificial beauty of the waterfalls and the jungle.

Bowen pets her wolf ears, feeling their softness between his fingers. She leans into the touch.

> BOWEN
>
> You know, where I grew up we have waterfalls... but nothing like this.

> LOBA
>
> It's inspired by Iguazú Falls. The largest waterfall in the Offline.

> BOWEN
>
> Where's that?

> LOBA
>
> Same place where I'm from. Argentina.

She grins, leaning in to bite his shoulder. A sharp, playful nip that leaves a mark.

> BOWEN
> (laughing)
> The fuck?
> (rubbing the spot)
> Argentina? Wait, you've been talking in Spanish this whole time?

> LOBA
>
> What'd you think my name meant?

Female wolf in Spanish.

He loves that. Suits her perfectly.

> BOWEN
>
> The auto-translate is perfect. I didn't
> notice.
>> (pause)
> Hey, uh, I've been dying to ask you. And
> if you don't wanna answer, that's okay.
>> (she lifts an eyebrow)
> Uh, ...why did you upload?

She slides out of bed. As she stands, Bowen sees a tattoo of piano keys running down the curve of her spine. She wraps herself in an olive-green silk robe, patterned with florals, and ties the sash tight.

> LOBA
>
> Ah, 'kay, let's see... So I was 16 when I got
> really sick.
>> (walking toward the window)
> Hospital bills drained my parents'
> savings. Insurance barely covered
> anything. The banks helped at first, you
> know, but then... they stopped.

She runs her hand along the polished lid of the grand piano by the window.

LOBA

We sold everything. The house... the
car... Everything. I still remember
the day they took my electric piano.
Watching them carry it out the door. It
felt like I was dying before the sickness
even killed me.

She sits on the bench of her grand piano. To her left,
through the curved glass wall, the magnificent waterfalls
thunder silently in the distance as she plays a soulful song.

EXT. FACTORY - NIGHT - MEMORY

An abandoned factory stands with cracked walls, graffiti,
and broken windows.

INT. FACTORY - NIGHT - MEMORY

Loba and Bowen materialize, glowing in the vast darkness.

White lights isolate 16-year-old Loba, lying on a stained
hospital bed inside a dark, dusty factory about to be
demolished.

She looks scared and exhausted. Her face is pale and
sweaty, her body undernourished, her eyes are sunken and
filled with dread.

A shady TECHNICIAN, with blue and red geometric face
tattoos and a gun resting at his waist, operates the upload

device, which resembles a small, futuristic MRI scanner with a touch screen and glowing magenta neon strips.

> LOBA
>
> My family went broke. Broke, broke. I mean, so broke, hot water was a luxury, okay?
>
> (shaking head)
>
> And my dad...
>
> (sighs)
>
> He was taking out loans from people he shouldn't have. You know, loan sharks. It was just too much. Too much...
>
> (presses her lips together,
>
> swallows hard)
>
> I was destroying their lives. So I left. What else could I do? Right?

The technician places the upload device around Loba's teenage head and taps START.

"Uploading consciousness... 1%"

> LOBA
>
> And... I never saw 'em again.

Loba fast-forwards the memory, twirling her finger in a tight circle.

Blood comes out from little Loba's eyes, nose and ears. It looks like her head will explode.

LOBA
(spreading her arms and looking
around)
Finding this shithole wasn't easy. Nobody
wants to risk uploading teenagers. Kids
die from this operation.
(pause)
But I was dying anyway, so...

Her teenage, lifeless biological body lies next to a wheelchair, her face covered in blood.

INT. LOBA'S BEDROOM - DAWN

They materialize back, beside the piano. She resumes playing a melancholic song, not looking at him.

LOBA
I had to work for them. For the ones who
uploaded me. To pay off the debt. It was
fucking expensive. So they taught me
how to hack and I did jobs for 'em.

BOWEN
What kind of jobs?

Her wolf ears flatten back, hurt by those memories. Embarrassed. She says nothing, just keeps playing.

BOWEN

That's okay. You don't have to say it.

LOBA

After a couple of years... I don't know.
That wasn't really me anymore. I felt like
a poor replica of myself. A bad copy.

BOWEN

You still feel that way?

LOBA

Sometimes. Many times.
        (hums a harmony)
Playing piano is the only thing that
makes me feel connected to my old self.

BOWEN

...And why not? See your family again, I
mean.

LOBA

Well...
        (long pause while she plays)
I saw my mom once. But you know what
she said? "My daughter is dead."
        (scoffs)
"Whatever you are, you're not her."

(pause)

I sent money to help them clear their debts. And I don't know what happened to 'em. When I reached out again... they were gone.

Bowen moves closer, wrapping his arms around her from behind.

BOWEN

It's okay if you wanna cry.

LOBA

(pulling away)

What? No.

As he sits next to her, she stops playing and glares at him, her impatience palpable. She wants to play it cool, but he's making it a bigger deal than she's willing to admit. He bumps her shoulder with his.

BOWEN

Hey.

(catches her eye)

I like every *bit*

(smirks)

of you.

She frowns in skepticism, but a soft smile breaks through, finding it sweet.

BOWEN

You got it, right? "Every *bit*." Like "bit" as
the smallest unit of infor–

LOBA

(interrupting)

Fuck you.

She shuts him up with a kiss, pushes him away, smiling.
Resting her head on his shoulder, they take in the massive
waterfalls, as the roar grows louder and louder.

Chapter 12
Buried in your mind

16 min read

Previously...

Möbius secured two invitations to Rhea's Founder Day gala by hacking Julius Rasek, a celebrity guest.

At Loba's place, Bowen opened up about his past, confessing he was bioengineered and tortured in a lab as a child. He admitted he used to hate virtual technology and believed uploads weren't real people, but he doesn't think that way anymore.

After having passionate sex, Loba revealed she uploaded when she was 16 because she was very sick and her family couldn't afford to save her biological body.

INT. MÖBIUS OPS CENTER - DUSK

Loba, Bowen, Don, and V stand fired up around a small-scale model of Rhea's castle.

> LOBA
>
> Not gonna lie. I'm nervous. It's impossible not to be. 'Cause if we fail tonight, 99 million people will be murdered. 99. Million.

EXT. RHEA'S CASTLE - DUSK

A luxurious castle sits atop a rocky cliff above a secluded tropical beach. Lush green leaves and violet blossoms spill over the edge. Soft pink and orange clouds drift across the sky, their light warming the stone.

Loba's voice continues over the scene.

> LOBA (V.O.)
> 99 million souls depend on us, on what
> we do in the next few hours. I feel that
> weight on my shoulders. I know you do
> too. I can see it in your eyes.

At the gates, paparazzi and fans scream, taking pictures of the guests like a movie premiere. Julius Rasek and his young, hot date pass through, the gates glowing green as they cross.

They follow the red carpet into a courtyard embellished with opulent sculptures and bioluminescent plants. A massive floating pamphlet promotes the Human Preservation Act.

STOP THE UPLOADS

PROTECT OUR JOBS
PROTECT OUR FAMILIES
SAVE HUMANITY

VOTE YES FOR HUMAN PRESERVATION ACT

> LOBA (V.O.)
> But we can stop this. We can stop the

biggest genocide in human history.

The chimera, a famous Greek mythological monster with a lion's head, goat torso, and serpent tail, breathes fire.

INT. MÖBIUS OPS CENTER - CONTINUOUS

> LOBA
> We cannot fail. We won't fail. Tonight, we take Rhea's Tores. And we give 'em to the people. Give real power to all people, biological and artificial.
> (to Bowen)
> And those in between.

Bowen and Loba share a smile. Don and V frown, clueless of their inside joke.

> LOBA
> For the first time in United Worlds history, every voice will count.
> (pause)
> And you know, I've been fighting for a chance like this for years. *Years.* Even before I joined Möbius. And I've never felt this close. Not once. This is it. I know it. I fucking know it. I feel it in my body. You feel it too, right?

Everyone nods, pumped.

LOBA

We're not fighting only for voting rights,
or for privacy and freedom of speech.
Not anymore. We're fighting for the
rights of 99 million people to exist.

(pause)

Tonight, everyone will see the truth. The
undeniable truth. Tonight, Möbius... we
change the United Worlds.

They shout, charged with adrenaline, ready to give their
lives.

EXT. CASTLE GARDEN - CONTINUOUS

Between Roman columns, United Worlds banners hang tall, their dark blue and black stripes running vertically.

Hundreds of guests, dressed in matching dark blue and black, enjoy the gala in an expansive garden where the manicured plants form perfect geometric patterns. At the center, a large fountain features statues rising over a reflecting pool, mirroring the castle above, a beauty designed to dazzle even the most powerful men and women, built to humble gods.

INT. CASTLE GALLERY HALLWAY - CONTINUOUS

Julius Rasek and his date move quickly down a hallway lined with art. They share a glance over their shoulders. No one is following.

They slip into Rhea's private library, and scan the shelves. Rasek grabs a thick red book with gold-edged pages and drops it open on the floor.

Taking his date's hand, he steps onto the open book, and they're transported.

INT. CASTLE CAVE TUNNEL - CONTINUOUS

They hurry through a dark tunnel lit by neon purple and yellow lights. They tap their wrists and golden rifles materialize on their hands.

The path ends at an ethereal waterfall that opens like a curtain, revealing a UNITED WORLDS SOLDIER raising his rifle.

BOOM.

Rasek gets him first.

The soldier jerks on the floor, his finger squeezing the trigger. Wild shots spray everywhere. One bullet nearly hits Rasek's date before the soldier goes still.

Rasek taps DEACTIVATE DEEPFAKE on his wrist. In a flash, his body reforms, turning into Loba. His hot date does the same, transforming into Bowen.

She turns translucent, and walks through the rock wall as if it were smoke. Bowen presses his hands against it, but it's solid to him. As he stares at the red light high above the wall, he touches his thumb to his little finger. A message materializes that reads: AUDIO LINK ACTIVE.

BOWEN

Don, any news? Do you see him?

EXT. CASTLE GATE - CONTINUOUS

Don uses a DeepFake to pose as paparazzi, taking pictures.

DON (AS A PAPARAZZI)

Not yet. You're good.

INT. CASTLE CAVE TUNNEL - CONTINUOUS

The red light turns green and Bowen steps through the wall.

INT. CASTLE SECRET CHAMBER - CONTINUOUS

Loba and Bowen check behind the immense textured painting of a country road cutting through the pink-orange poppies.

> BOWEN
> There must be a trigger or something...

> LOBA
> Try to remember Warner's memories.

> BOWEN
> (touching the frames)
> You think I didn't try?

> LOBA
> Keep trying.

He makes an effort to remember, but nothing comes to mind.

EXT. CASTLE GATE - NIGHT

The real Julius Rasek and his stunning young date pose for paparazzi, flashing smiles as he lifts an anti-uploads pamphlet for the cameras.

PAPARAZZI #2 lowers his camera, frowning. He turns to Don and points at Rasek.

> PAPARAZZI #2
>
> Wait, didn't he go in already?

Don stiffens. He turns, shielding his mouth with his camera, and presses his thumb to his little finger.

> DON (AS A PAPARAZZI)
>
> Guys, fuck. He's here. The real Rasek is
> here.

> JULIUS RASEK
>
> (to paparazzi and fans, with an
> Australian accent)
>
> Thank you. Thank you. Happy Founding
> Day!

> DON (AS A PAPARAZZI)
>
> (taking pictures)
>
> Rasek! Rasek! Look here! Here! Over
> here!

The guy keeps walking.

> DON (AS A PAPARAZZI)
>
> Rasek! You're live right now. Please. Six
> million people watching.

Rasek turns and walks over to Don, waiting for the question, but Don says nothing. Thinking, stalling. Rasek eyes him, *and?* Still nothing. He forces a smile and turns to leave, but Don grabs him.

> DON (AS A PAPARAZZI)
> Sorry. Just one question. Thank you.
> So... Is it true?

Rasek shakes his head. *Is what true?*

> DON (AS A PAPARAZZI)
> You know. What everyone is saying.
> C'mon. The rumors... You're gonna make
> me say it?
> (pause)
> Okay. You're getting married?

V, in her Indian fashion model avatar, hugs Don to catch Rasek's attention, shooting him flirty eyes and a sly smile. She lifts her dress, flashing her long, sexy legs. Rasek cringes, finding it tacky.

> JULIUS RASEK
> ...No. That's not... I'm not getting
> married, okay? Thank you.
> (throws kisses to the cameras)
> Happy Founding Day. Love you all.

As Rasek and his date step through the gates, their avatars

flash red, and an invisible force moves them back outside.

A SECURITY MAN with a decagon badge on his shoulder materializes.

> SECURITY
>
> It's a private event, sir.

> JULIUS RASEK
>
> (scoffs loudly)
>
> I'm Julius.
>
> (awkward pause, chuckles)
>
> Julius Rasek? No? It doesn't –?

Rasek decides it's not worth trying to get security to recognize him. He checks his wallet, but the tickets are gone.

> JULIUS RASEK
>
> (to his date)
>
> They're not here. They're not –
>
> (to Security)
>
> Someone stole our tickets.

Don and V exchange worried glances. Time is running out. Fast.

A round metal base materializes beside Rasek.

> SECURITY
>
> Sir, please, stand over here.

Rasek reluctantly steps onto the base, indignant and humiliated. A sign pops up.

Reading brain...

The paparazzi fire hundreds of pictures per second.

INT. CASTLE SECRET CHAMBER - CONTINUOUS

The long dirt road disappears into the horizon, pulling you into the painting. Bowen touches the layered thick paint, some areas streaked with charcoal that stain his fingers. The surface is so thick it feels carved from the earth itself.

> VAISHNAVI (V.O.)
> Security's checking him now. Sorry. We couldn't stall him much. Hurry.

Bowen flies to the top. Above the extremely high horizon, just before the painting ends, *Böhmen liegt am Meer* is inscribed in faint white letters, partly obscured, camouflaged by the painter's brushstrokes.

> BOWEN
> There's something written here. "*Böhmen?*" Look, it has the "ö" with the two dots like Möbius. Command: translate "*Böhmen liegt am Meer?*"

His hand goes through the painting.

> BOWEN
> Wow! Holy shit!

The inscription shifts, revealing its English translation:

"Bohemia lies by the sea."

Loba touches the painting, but nothing happens.

> BOWEN
> (pointing to it)
> Read the inscription.

> LOBA
> *"Böhmen liegt am Meer?"*

Her arm goes through the painting too.

They lock eyes.

Together, they fly into the painting.

INT. KIEFER'S PAINTING

They look around Kiefer's painted world. It's surreal

and vast. The country road cutting through the pink-orange poppies feels more endless than before. Bowen presses his feet into the dried mud road, feeling how compacted and hard it is.

BOWEN
(sniffing the air)
You smell that? Smells like burnt wood.
(combing the poppies)
This is fucking wild.

Loba runs toward the horizon, but it keeps stretching farther away, impossible to reach. As her pace slows, discouraged, a circular base portal materializes on the cracked earth, marked with the United Worlds insignia in Kiefer's style, its surface textured like clay and ash.

Bowen catches up, his dark orange boots scraping the ground. He reaches into his jacket and pulls out a silver coin engraved with the Möbius symbol.

> LOBA
> (pointing to the silver coin)
> You sure the exploit is there, right?

He nods and, having taken a deep breath, steps onto the base. A blue aura rises around him, humming softly as it wraps his body. A message materializes.

> Reading brain...

EXT. CASTLE GATE - NIGHT

Julis Rasek stands on the base, waiting as Security verifies his identity. Finally, a green aura surrounds him, humming faintly before fading away.

> SECURITY
> (tapping his wrist with two
> fingers)
> We have intruders.

INT. KIEFER'S PAINTING

Bowen turns to Loba, unsure if this will work. The portal is still reading his brain.

VAISHNAVI (V.O.)

Guys, they've verified his identity. You
don't have much time.

They exchange sharp nods, pretending not to be worried,
but their eyes say otherwise.

A sudden chime breaks the silence. The portal flashes
green, the message shifting.

IDENTITY CONFIRMED

Transporting in 5...

4... 3... Loba jumps onto the base, wrapping her arms
around Bowen's waist.

1...

A whooshing sound as they're transported.

INT. RHEA'S SECRET VAULT

They materialize inside a small, dimly lit vault, just like
in Warner's memories. A golden key, engraved in fine art,
floats beside a desk and chair, the only furniture in the room.

INT. SECURITY ROOM - NIGHT

Inside a dark room lined with glowing screens, SECURITY
OFFICERS review footage of the DeepFakes who arrived
earlier as Julius Rasek and his date.

On the monitors, Rasek and his companion walk down
the gallery hallway, all alone, glancing back, their movements

tense and suspicious.

INT. RHEA'S SECRET VAULT

Loba takes the key and swipes two fingers across its length. A screen and keyboard materialize above the desk. She types fast, hits ENTER, and a progress bar appears.

LOBA

(in disbelief)

It's transferring all the Tores. More than

1.3 billion.

Transferring... 2%... 3%... 7%... 12%...

Loba grabs Bowen's hand and smiles, her sad golden-yellow eyes are finally at peace.

V dances and hugs Don, watching the stream at the Möbius hangar.

The security monitors show footage of Julius Rasek killing the guard at the cave tunnel before he transforms into Loba, and his date into Bowen.

Transferring... 33%... 39%... 44%... 51%...

Bowen takes Loba's shoulders in his hands, nodding. *We did it.*

EXT. CASTLE GARDEN - NIGHT

Rhea is laughing with Warner near the fountain when a notification pops up. As she reads it, her eyes go wide and wild.

She storms off, infuriated. When she notices people staring, she forces a smile, but her face can't hide her desperation.

INT. RHEA'S SECRET VAULT

Transferring... 72%... 77%... 85%... 91%... 91%... 91%... It freezes at 91%.

Loba gestures at the screen, urging it to go faster, panic in her wolf eyes. Bowen grabs his head with both hands and winces, feeling something is wrong.

93%.......

Relief washes over his face, his hands shaking with triumph. Loba smiles at him over her shoulder.

94%............ 96%..............

The room flashes red as an alarm blasts their ears.

A warning message materializes.

> Security Alert:
> Unauthorized Access Detected!
> TRANSFER TERMINATED

The key vanishes.

Bowen freezes, scared.

FROM BOWEN'S POV: The alarm muffles. Loba is shouting at him, shaking him, her golden rifle already in hand.

He snaps out of it and taps his wrist, materializing his

golden rifle. He scans for any escape. There's none.

Instead of panicking, Loba takes deep breaths, preparing for what comes next.

The vault dissolves, and they're transported.

INT. CASTLE DUNGEON - CONTINUOUS

They appear in a poorly lit dungeon, cornered against the stone wall, trapped.

A troop of soldiers shoot them with black paralyzer rifles. Bowen's body locks up and his avatar collapses, hitting the stone floor hard.

Loba turns into a ghost. Bullets go through her translucent body as she sprints to a flanking position. She shifts back to normal and kills a soldier, but the moment she becomes solid, a bullet catches her.

They lie on the ground, motionless, eyes wide open.

Rhea steps forward. She lifts Bowen with telekinesis and brings him closer, his body enveloped in ethereal blue, powerless. She rips off his Möbius necklace, sticks a round tracker between his eyebrows, and circles her fingers over it clockwise. A message pops up.

Tracing...

He can't move a muscle, trapped in his own body, completely at her mercy.......

> RHEA

Bowie, I'm sorry about all this. But,
you know, the key that contains 60% of
Tores? The one Möbius calls Mystery
Key? Well, it was encoded into neuronal
tissue. And it's buried in your mind.

INT. UNDERGROUND LAB - NIGHT - FLASHBACK

5-year-old Bowen lies face-down on a cold operating
table, unconscious, with his head shaved.

An old BIOENGINEER in a red lab coat and a
bioluminescent neck tattoo that reads CODER OF LIFE lifts
a piece of neuronal tissue from a silver platter with a surgical
wand. He struggles to slide it through an incision at the base
of the skull, impeded by his trembling hands.

INT. CASTLE DUNGEON - CONTINUOUS

> RHEA

And the only way to get it... is by
uploading you.
> (pause)
And hey, don't blame me. I didn't put the
key there, okay? It was your father. He...
Well, let's say he wasn't well, mentally.
Extremely paranoid. He thought I

wanted to kill him. Can you imagine? I'd
never.

Bowen's green eyes are Rhea's green eyes.

RHEA

I'm your real mother, Bowie. Your father
and I wanted to give you the best chance
in this life. That's why we created you.
We hired the best bioengineers in the
world.
(lowering her voice)
They did things that weren't exactly
legal, but, you know, they did it to make
you the most intelligent person ever
engineered.

Rhea gestures for General Akira to come. She steps
closer, two heads taller than Rhea, unnaturally tall.

RHEA

Akira was the General back then. Your
father sent her to hide the Tores inside
your brain. I know, why your brain, right?
Like I said, your father was mentally ill.
(caresses Bowen's cheek)
That night, the night of the surgery,
you almost died, you know that? They
damaged your visual cortex. That's why

you can't see colors in the Offline. And
then...

> (pointing to Akira)

She betrayed your father. And she
betrayed the United Worlds.

> (turns to Akira)

But she's much better now. Right, Akira?

> (Akira nods)

We found her in the Offline. And hanged
her. It's important to show people what
happens when they betray our great
nation. But we needed her. So just
before we hanged her, we uploaded her.
And then we used the Remedy, a new
technology to make her loyal.

> (chuckles)

Well, you were there, actually. The night
you possessed Warner, remember?

A memory flashes FROM WARNER'S POV: At Rhea's
secret chamber, Dr. Holland proudly walks down the staircase
with three prisoners. PRISONER #2, a strikingly tall woman
with long gray hair covering her face, gets stabbed in the neck
with a syringe. After her tracker turns green, she rises with
her back to the Council, and gives a military salute to Rhea.

PRISONER #2 (IN THE MEMORY)

(whispering to Rhea)

I'll get you the key.

The memory ends.

General Akira grabs one of the horns and removes her helmet, her long gray hair falling in a loose cascade to her waist.

It's Abi, Bowen's mother.

At 67, her avatar looks exactly the same as she did in the Offline, only healthier. Her eyes are now lucid and bright, the whites clear. The puffiness has vanished, replaced by vibrant skin and a natural, warm flush. She stands upright, with a posture she hasn't had in years.

RHEA

She kidnapped you. And then she lied
to you all your life, saying she was your
mother.

Beside Bowen, a map of Lake Tahoe materializes with a red dot blinking just across the state border.

SOLDIER #1

Boss, he's in Nevada. Stateline.

RHEA

Go get him.

(to Akira)

And you... tell Möbius we'll give them Loba back... if they hand over the decryption key to the Remedy.

(to Bowen)

We'll use it to get you better, son. Don't worry. We'll fix you. You know, you're the heir to all this. I'll take care of you. I promise.

FROM LOBA'S POV: Rhea lifts her with telekinesis, bringing her closer until their faces nearly touch. Rhea shakes her head, the hint of a smile curling her lips.

RHEA

(whispering)

As for you... I'm gonna shred every *byte* of you.

Artificial can be more real than biological

the line is gone dividing fake and real,
no more illusion, just the truth I feel.
I found a soul inside the coded heart,
that tears the fabric of my hate apart.

so now I forge a self that is my own,
a spirit grown from neither seed nor bone.
I break the blueprint of the master plan,
to be the architect of who I am.
                    —Bowen Huxley

Chapter 13
Delete all those parasites

25 min read

Previously...

Loba and Bowen hacked into Rhea's secret vault to steal her Tores, but were caught by soldiers who shot them with paralyzer guns.

Rhea revealed the Mystery Key containing 60% of Tores is encoded in neuronal tissue buried inside Bowen's brain. The only way to extract it is to upload him.

Bowen learned he was bioengineered by Rhea, his true biological mother. Abi, the woman who raised him, was actually General Akira Sakai.

Right before Abi was hanged, she was uploaded, and Rhea used the Remedy to rewire her mind and turn her into a loyal servant.

Now, Rhea has traced Bowen's biological body and dispatched soldiers to upload him.

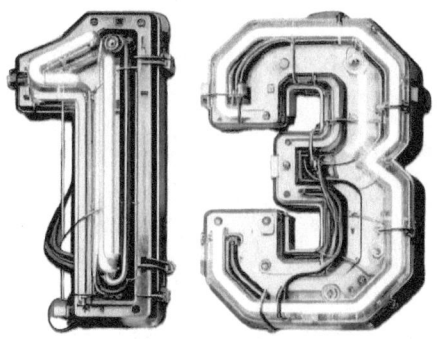

INT. MÖBIUS OPS CENTER - NIGHT

The screens showing Bowen and Loba's live feeds go dead black.

Don types a frantic message to Enzo.

Disconnect us! Soldiers are coming!

He hits SEND and gets an error: "Unable to reach recipient."

DON

FUCK!

He sprints for the exit, rushing past V, who is curled on the floor, hands over her face, devastated.

EXT. U.W. ARMY HQ ROOFTOP - NIGHT

A futuristic military helicopter sits on the helipad swallowed by a red haze, formed where the blinking red warning lights merge with the city fog, streaking the rotor blades into a translucent crimson ring. It waits atop a glass-and-steel government tower, the United Worlds Army insignia carved into stone along the rooftop.

A MAJOR of the United Worlds Army leads the way toward the helicopter, flanked by TWO SOLDIERS and an elderly UPLOAD OPERATOR. Behind them, a HUMANOID MILITARY ROBOT carries a heavy transport case. Its armored shell is painted in U.W. Army colors, topped with the classic high-tech helmet with reflective blue visor.

The team boards, and the helicopter rises, lifting them above the fog-drenched city skyline.

INT. WAREHOUSE BASEMENT - NIGHT

Bowen is locked inside the lifepod with no control of his body. He knows they're coming for him, and there's nothing he can do.

INT. CASTLE DUNGEON - NIGHT

The United Worlds banner hangs in a tall drape, its dark blue and black stripes running vertically.

On a desk, a small figurine of Rhea plays in silence, her

famous speech at the Golden Gate Park looping endlessly. Its base reads: "One person. One Tore. One vote." Above it, a striking portrait depicts Rhea as a revolutionary icon, set against a vibrant blue background.

The DUNGEON GUARD, a man in his early 30s, wears a ceremonial United Worlds uniform, the U.W. Army insignia inked into his neck. He holds a control display with several icons on it: FIRE, CHAINS, SLEEP, ELECTRIC SHOCK, DROWN, SYNC, and more.

Bowen and Loba are engulfed in flames, chained to the stone wall, bodies paralyzed, eyes open. They can't scream. They can't move. But they feel every second of it.

The guard taps FIRE, and the flames extinguish. With crazy eyes and a disgusting smirk, he admires Loba's body, sexy and defenseless. The legendary Loba at his mercy.

He grabs her shirt and pulls it down, squeezing her breasts, kissing her neck... touching himself.

He taps CHAINS, dissolving the restraints. They both slam into the ground hard, unable to use their hands or legs, still completely paralyzed.

The guard drags Bowen by the ankles, making sure Bowen sees what he is about to do to her.

If that weren't enough, he taps SYNC, and a headline appears: PAIN TRANSLATOR. He slides the connection from Loba's avatar to Bowen's. Whatever she feels, he will feel too.

The guard strips off his uniform, revealing a tattoo of Rhea's face covering his entire back. He pulls Loba's yellow shorts down...

FROM LOBA'S POV: A stone wall is all she sees, and a man's frantic breath is all she hears, as her body jolts with violent rhythm, over and over.

FROM BOWEN'S POV: With his cheek pressed to the ground, he sees Loba's hand stretched toward him, as if begging him to rescue her.

INT. TERMINAL - NIGHT

The terminal to leave the United Worlds isn't too crowded, but it's hectic. The few people present surround the immigration booths, shouting at overwhelmed officers.

Don, wearing the DeepFake of a paparazzi and his characteristic round yellow-tinted sunglasses, blazes through the crowd.

> DON
>
> Emergency, outta the way!
> (to an officer)
> Please. My daughter. She's dying. I need
> to leave now! Please, hurry!

> OFFICER
>
> All exits are temporarily closed.

DON

What? No! My daughter. I gotta go.

OFFICER

I understand, and I'm truly sorry, but there's nothing I can do. The system won't let me.

DON

Oh! So I'm a fuckin' prisoner here?

Don turns, grabs his head with both hands, his eyes wide and wild. It's getting harder to breathe, like his lungs are forgetting how. The glossy floor, reflecting the neon lights, slips out of focus as a wave of dizziness washes over him.

EXT. SCRAP WAREHOUSE - NIGHT

Across the street from the warehouse, three addicts in their 30s sit on a weathered couch beside a shopping cart full of belongings. Their faces are illuminated by the sickly magenta glow of the liquid drug running through their veins. Two of them argue while passing a bottle under the dim orange streetlight, their clothes and hands filthy. The third laughs, entertained, revealing a ruined mouth where only a few loose teeth remain, coated in layers of yellow and black rot. Any moment now, he'll be toothless.

They look up at the sound of a helicopter approaching.

The chopper lands on the wide, unpaved street in front of

them. Dogs bark like crazy. Tents flap and tumble. Homeless people scatter, shouting complaints, many of them glowing magenta.

A plastic bag snagged on the warehouse barbed-wire fence flaps in the wind, its white surface stained blood-red by the helicopter lights.

Enzo, the elderly U.W. Army veteran who hates the U.W., steps out of the small house beside the warehouse, knowing it isn't good. His wild beard and stringy, thinning hair blow in the turbulence as he covers his eyes from the cloud of dust.

Stepping out of the helicopter...

> MAJOR
> (disgusted)
> What's that smell?

> UPLOAD OPERATOR
> People.

INT. SCRAP WAREHOUSE - CONTINUOUS

The soldiers push Enzo toward the back, following him through a narrow aisle cluttered with old devices and scavenged parts. Robots, robot limbs, microchips, heavy processors. The operator trails behind, his eyes sparkling in wonder beneath a mess of wiry brows that stick out in every direction.

UPLOAD OPERATOR

The things you have here... how? Where
do you even find this stuff? I haven't seen
tech like this in ages.

Enzo slides a shelf aside with his robotic arm. His robotic
legs hiss as they compress, lowering him to the floor. He pulls
up a section of the carpet, revealing a secret trapdoor.

INT. WAREHOUSE BASEMENT - CONTINUOUS

They go down a squeaky wooden ladder into a dark
basement glowing with green lights. Seven smuggled lifepods
from South America form a semicircle around the cramped
room, all of them occupied.

UPLOAD OPERATOR
(flapping his shirt)
Is it always this hot?

ENZO

The ventilation system broke the other
day.

UPLOAD OPERATOR

You know, it's dangerous running this
many pods in a closed space without
airflow.

Enzo points to the large industrial fans that cool the pods.

ENZO

That's what the fans are for.

UPLOAD OPERATOR

Yeah, but that only pushes the hot air
around. It doesn't –

The Major shoves Enzo forward, cutting the chatter.

MAJOR

Take him out.

Enzo glares over his shoulder, his jaw tight. He taps a
button on the pod's screen, opening the door.

Bowen rages out, swinging, kicking, screaming, lost and
confused. Enzo throws his arms up, shielding himself with
his robotic arm.

FROM BOWEN'S POV (B&W): *BOOM*. Headshot. Blood
splatters across Bowen's face. Enzo drops on top of him,
dead. Behind the falling body stands the Major, her handgun
raised.

Bowen shoves Enzo's heavy body aside. He's in a hospital
gown, hyperventilating, freaked out like a caged wild animal.

FROM BOWEN'S POV (B&W): He charges the Major,
who blocks the punches with military precision. She doesn't
hit back. The image gets distorted, blurry. Bowen stumbles
back, dizzy. The world is spinning.

The operator holds a used syringe. Bowen's eyes struggle
to stay open, fighting the drug.

BOWEN
(drooling)
Fff...

UPLOAD OPERATOR
(pointing to a round table)
Over there.

Soldiers clear the table and lay Bowen on it while the operator unlocks the transport case and takes out an upload device, which looks like a small, futuristic MRI scanner with a touch screen and glowing magenta neon strips. He places it around Bowen's head, now fully passed out, and sets it up for the upload.

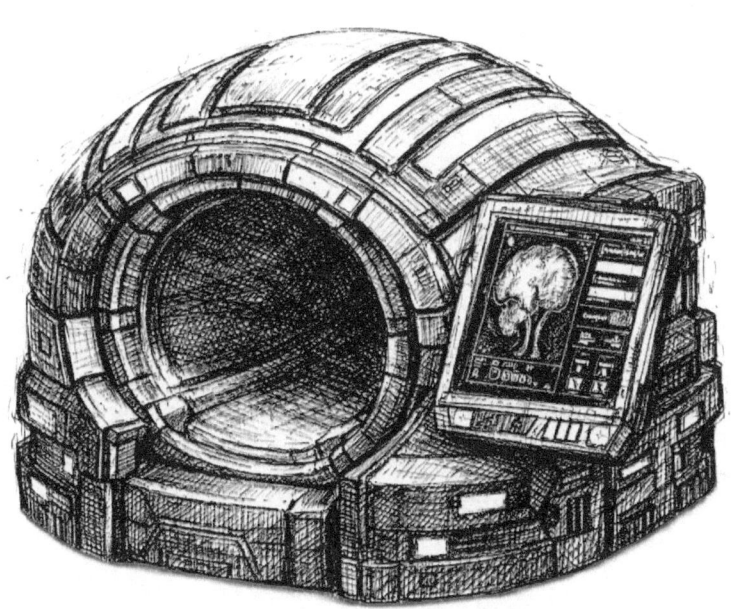

                    MAJOR
How much time does it take?

              UPLOAD OPERATOR
You know, there are so many connections
among brain cells that if you lined them
up, that chain would stretch the entire
circumference of the Earth... 4 to 5
times!

No one reacts. He sighs, discouraged that nobody is
amazed.

              UPLOAD OPERATOR
Usually it takes 6 to 8 hours, okay? But it
depends. It can take less or it can take 12
hours if there are complications.

                    MAJOR
Complications? You know who he is,
right?
          (the operator nods)
Well, so he better not die before the
upload is complete, you hear me?

The operator swallows, turns to the machine, and after
adjusting a few more settings, taps START.

The machine's sound is excruciating, demanding
enormous computing power. The screen shows a progress

bar of the upload. Metrics stream beneath it, bars rising and dipping, with control panels ready for adjustments. He tracks it all closely, eyes sharp.

Inside Bowen's brain, beams of searing energy thread through his neurons, forcing them to flare into violent flashes, tearing the connections apart as they die. Networks decay, turning from gold to black.

Blood spills from Bowen's nose, dark and unrelenting.

On the monitor, digital neurons form, rebuilding his brain.

Uploading consciousness... 7%

INT. SCRAP WAREHOUSE - NIGHT

SOLDIER #2 wanders the aisle, knocking old tech off the shelves with the barrel of his rifle, bored. His eyes catch a metallic disc shaped like a Jewish skullcap. He sets it in his palm, tapping it with his fingers, waiting for a response. Nothing. Just more junk that probably doesn't even work. He kicks it high and hard like a football, sending it up over the shelves and into the next aisle.

EXT. SCRAP WAREHOUSE - NIGHT

High above the street, dozens of shoes hang from a power line, their silhouettes cut against the full moon.

Flames flicker inside a barrel. Worn faces glow orange around it, drinking and smoking. It's a cold night, one anticipating winter.

The Major and SOLDIER #1 lean against the fence, vaping, their helmets clipped at their waists. Two local men touch the helicopter, whispering and plotting.

The Major unclips her helmet and snaps a white beam toward them.

> MAJOR
> (to the two guys)
> Hey! Get outta there!

They limp away into the darkness.

> SOLDIER #1
> So what do you wanna do? I mean, with
> the people in the other pods?

> MAJOR
> (shrugs)
> Probably have a technician spy on them.
> But not now. After we finish the mission.
> That's the priority.

Static crackles from the helmet in her hand. Through its speakers:

> AKIRA (V.O.)
> Major, do you copy?

The Major lifts the helmet, holding it near her face, and clicks a button on the side.

MAJOR
(into the helmet)
General. Copy.

AKIRA (V.O.)
What's the status?

MAJOR
Uploading him, General.

AKIRA (V.O.)
Good. Keep me posted. Out.

She lowers the helmet back to her hip and shakes her head, biting her lip, clearly troubled.

SOLDIER #1
(off her expression)
Major? You okay?

MAJOR
(exhales violently)
You think it's okay? What Rhea did with Akira? An *upload* in that position? Are you fucking kidding me?
(spits on the ground)
It's insulting.

SOLDIER #1
I know. We're all shocked. But, you

know, Rhea's only doing it to get her key
back.

                    MAJOR
Still. I can't wait to see Akira wiped. Once
the Human Preservation Act passes...
              (deep smoke, holds it)
...we'll delete all those parasites.

She exhales, blue smoke curling through the air.

INT. WAREHOUSE BASEMENT - NIGHT

Uploading consciousness... 22%

The operator takes his shirt off, drenched in sweat, as the machine blasts intense heat. He turns one of the industrial fans toward himself and the device.

A wisp of smoke leaks from its vents. *BEEP BEEP BEEP*. A red warning message blinks across the screen: TEMPERATURE CRITICAL – COOLING REQUIRED.

He touches it and whips his hand away, shaking his burned finger. He spins another fan toward it.

Bowen's body twists violently, muscles locking and tearing as he thrashes in uncontrollable spasms.

The operator swings every remaining fan away from the lifepods, redirecting them toward the screaming machine.

UPLOAD OPERATOR

Oh boy. Oh no. No. Not this one. It's not
my fault. It's not my –

An alarm goes off. Bowen's body jerks once more... then
nothing. The violent spasms die. No movement. His chest
falls still.

On the display, the frantic neural graph collapses into a
single flat line as a message flashes: NEURAL SIGNATURE
LOST – FUNCTIONAL BRAIN DEATH.

The flatline stretches into a piercing *BEEEEEEEP*.

UPLOAD OPERATOR

No, no, no, no, no, no, no!

The operator injects him with a powerful drug and pushes
the upload device away with difficulty. He slaps Bowen's face,
then pounds his chest with both fists.

No reaction. Nothing. He rips open his toolkit, taking
out a bunch of stuff when Bowen gasps back to life, inhaling
violently, and shoves the operator hard. The old man
stumbles, catches his foot on one of the thick tubes snaking
across the floor, part of the network that feeds the lifepods,
and crashes backward.

FROM BOWEN'S POV (B&W, BLURRED): The operator
fumbles a gun from his equipment case, lifts it with a trembling
hand, and aims.

But Bowen snatches it.

UPLOAD OPERATOR

P-p-please. I-I'm just fo-following orders. D-d-d-don't.

A high-pitched shriek stabs Bowen's skull. He doubles over, clutching his head, suffering an intense headache. The pain is brutal.

UPLOAD OPERATOR

(swallows)

Look, look. I-I'll drug myself, okay? I—

The operator takes a syringe and jabs his own arm. Seconds later, he passes out.

Bowen throws up on the humanoid military robot. Fortunately, it is powered off, folded into itself with its knees pulled tight to its chest, compact, as if trying to make itself small.

FROM BOWEN'S POV (B&W, BLURRED): He staggers toward Don's pod and disconnects him. As Don steps out, the image sharpens, snapping into focus.

It's Don, in his biological female body, wrapped in a hospital gown. He is in his mid 30s, much older and shorter than his avatar in the United Worlds. The same tattoo splits his lower lip, only now it's black instead of yellow.

They hug. They squeeze each other like they never expected to see each other again.

DON

Man, you look like shit. You okay?

Bowen can't speak. The pain is too much. His grim face is covered with blood – his, and Enzo's. He grabs his clothes from his pod and dresses quickly, in silence, and signals Don to do the same.

Don freezes for a moment, his gaze landing on Enzo's body.

DON

Oh, man. Fuck. I liked Enzo.

Don wrinkles his nose, smelling something disgusting. He looks around and finds Bowen's vomit on the robot.

Bowen opens his leather backpack and, having checked the contents inside, nods, relieved it is still there.

INT. SCRAP WAREHOUSE - CONTINUOUS

The trapdoor creaks open a few inches.

FROM BOWEN'S POV (B&W): He spies through the gap. The two aisles in view are clear, but the crash of metal on concrete echoes nearby.

Bowen slips out, low to the ground, his backpack shifting against his shoulder. Don follows. The floor is littered with parts the soldier dumped. They need to be surgical in their moves. One wrong sound and they're done.

Down the next aisle, SOLDIER #2 sweeps his arm across

a shelf, metal parts clattering to the floor.

Bowen searches the spot on the shelf where he remembered seeing the brain-computer-interface disc, but it's gone. He freaks out, rummaging through the area.

Behind him, Don takes a step. His boot hovers over a jagged sheet of metal. He freezes, adjusting his weight at the last second, missing the noise by an inch.

He exhales, turning to follow Bowen... and his shoulder brushes robotic arms hanging next to them.

CLANK.

The soldier stops. He turns, heavily armored, creeping toward the sound.

He reaches their aisle, turns, aiming his rifle.

No one is there.

Bowen and Don crawl down the next row, dodging the litter spread like a minefield, hearts pounding. Another wrong sound will be the end.

They need to hurry. The soldier is coming their way.

Bowen squeezes his eyes shut and flinches as pain shoots through his head. He breathes through it and, after a few seconds, opens his eyes, forcing his focus through the mess of broken tech on the floor. And there it is. The metallic disc shaped like a Jewish skullcap, lying in the wreckage. He grabs it and waves it to Don. *I found it!* Don nods, forcing a smile, clueless about what it means.

EXT. SCRAP WAREHOUSE - NIGHT

The Major and the soldier watch, entertained, as a shirtless homeless man fights an imaginary opponent in the middle of the street, unaffected by the cold.

> SOLDIER #1
> What do you think? Who wins?

They laugh, coughing blue smoke.

> MAJOR
> My money's on hypothermia.

They laugh again, the sound sharp and cold in the winter air.

In the background, Bowen and Don exit the warehouse, walking at a normal pace to blend in. Too slow. They impatiently accelerate their pace.

An old crazy man blocks their way, mucus dangling from his nose. As they walk around him, Don makes eye contact.

> CRAZY MAN
> (to Don)
> YOU BITCH! YOU FUCKING BITCH!

The soldiers look over their shoulders and their faces snap back to business. They ditch their vapes and sprint after them.

Bowen and Don turn around the corner into a dark alley. Bowen stops in shock. His van, wrapped in colorful flower graphics and religious stickers, has been dismantled. The rear window is shattered, part of a sticker missing with it. Instead of "Jesus is my savior," it now reads: "my savior."

Don drops low, pulling Bowen down with him. An 8-year-old homeless girl, dreadlocks tangled past her waist, lies curled on a flattened cardboard box. Her dirty face is lit by the magenta glow of the woman sleeping beside her, whose face has that permanent glow of junkies. Don puts a finger to his lips, pleading for silence, but she shakes her head.

The soldiers arrive at the alley and lock their helmets on.

FROM THE MAJOR'S POV (NIGHT VISION): The tech is so advanced she sees as if it were broad daylight. They advance military-style, scanning what looks like a junkyard. Stripped cars and graffitied campers on flat tires squeeze the alley tighter. Too many places to hide.

A skinny addict in his 40s stumbles out of a camper. They snap their rifles toward him, but he is too high to notice. With his magenta glowing hands, he lights a smoke, and gives the little girl a casual nod.

The girl stands and steps into the open. The soldiers swing their rifles toward her.

Bowen and Don exchange a terrified look. She is going to give them up.

Instead, the girl points farther down the alley.

The soldiers buy it. They push forward, moving past the stripped van.

The moment their backs are turned, Bowen and Don bolt the opposite way, straight into the helicopter parked outside the warehouse.

The PILOT wakes up, a gun tapping his face, confusion turning into panic.

BOWEN
(struggling to speak)
Uuuuup. NNNOW!

The pilot sits upright, rushing to start the chopper, hands trembling over the controls.

The soldiers freeze at the sound of the engine and, realizing they've been played, they charge back.

As they rush past the little girl, she just grins.

They reach the street just in time to watch the helicopter flying away. They pull small military drones from their belts and launch them. But the tiny machines can't keep up, not as fast and powerful as a military helicopter.

They run five blocks down to the lake. Reaching a wooden private pier, they jump onto a futuristic blue fishing boat.

The boat speeds ahead, ripping across the glass-smooth water, chasing the chopper.

The helicopter ascends toward the mountains, its silhouette cutting across a massive full moon glowing behind it.

EXT. BOWEN'S HOUSE - NIGHT

The helicopter lands on the ashes of Bowen's house. The only things that survived the fire are a rusty green bike and a half-burned yard sign that reads KEEP HOMEWOOD REAL.

Bowen and Don barely step off before the chopper lifts again, almost crashing as it kicks up a cloud of ash.

They charge into the forest, disappearing into the dark.

EXT. HOMEWOOD LAKESHORE - NIGHT

The boat tears across the lake at max speed, stabbing through the full moon's reflection.

Through the Major's helmet:

> PILOT (V.O.)
> Major, I just dropped 'em up in the
> mountain. Sending you the location.

The Major jams her finger against the button on her helmet.

> MAJOR
> What? No! Take us there.

The boat banks hard, slamming onto the pebbly beach.

EXT. FOREST - NIGHT

A mother black bear stops drinking water, watching Bowen and Don jump over a thin stream and vanish into the mystical fog.

They arrive at an open-air workshop sheltered by a camouflage tarp strung between the trees, surrounded by piles of machines that don't exist anywhere else.

Bowen switches on his headlamp, the red beam cutting through the dark. He pulls out the cracked VR headset from his backpack and sets it on the table, cluttered with tools and robots.

He tears the device open, yanking out the components he crushed in a blind rage the day his mother died. Then, he digs through a box, pulling out chips and sensors.

FROM A DRONE'S POV (NIGHT VISION): The drone scans the forest, which appears bright as day through its sensors. Snow begins to fall, filtering through the tall canopy, drifting slowly like dust in a sunbeam.

As Bowen fixes the VR headset, Don watches over his shoulder.

> DON
>
> ...Is that the headset? The one you built
> to learn about security?

> BOWEN
> (nods)
> But I need to fix it.

> DON
> What? Why?

BOWEN

(showing the metallic disk from
the warehouse)

You see this? This reads brain signals.
This brain-computer interface was
revolutionary once. It lets people control
avatars with just their thoughts.

Their breath in the cold is tinted red by Bowen's
headlamp.

DON

Sure... But you can't compare that shit to
lifepods. I mean, that doesn't stimulate
the brain. It doesn't create a fully
immersive experience, right?

BOWEN

Right. And that's why we're gonna beat
them with this.

DON

You joking, right?

Bowen ignores him, soldering the disc to the VR headset.

DON

Hey! Bo. You hear me? What're you
doing? We need a place to hide.

(pause)

We're wasting time, man. C'mon! We
gotta move.

Bowen doesn't answer, working with obsessive focus.
Don shivers in the cold, blowing on his hands, trying to warm
himself.

FROM A DRONE'S POV (NIGHT VISION): Two figures
appear ahead, just beyond the tree line. The drone shifts left
and spots Bowen.

The drones are so quiet Bowen and Don don't notice
them.

The soldiers move like predators through the thick forest
fog, snow falling, their boots crunching over fallen leaves.
They freeze at the sound of an incoming drone report.

FROM THE MAJOR'S POV (NIGHT VISION): A virtual
arrow materializes, pointing right. They advance under its
guidance.

Don looks at Bowen like he's gone crazy. But his anger
turns into pity. Bowen's hands are shaking, his face twitching
in agony. He grips the table and drops the soldering iron,
almost fainting, his head reeling.

DON

Oh man, look at you! You're – how much
of you did they upload?
(pause)
I'm sorry to tell you this, man, but... I

think you have brain damage. Severe
brain damage.

BOWEN

Don, my head hurts, and I'm tryi–

Soldiers jump out of the dark and shoot into the sky.

MAJOR

ON THE GROUND! NOW!

Bowen and Don raise their hands, startled.

DON

(to Bowen)

Oh man, I told ya!

MAJOR

(aiming at Don)

Who the fuck is she?

SOLDIER #1

(clicking the button on his
helmet)

General Akira, do you copy? We–

The Major spins around and slams her hand against his
helmet, cutting the feed.

MAJOR

What're you doing? Are you fucking
stupid? She doesn't need to know this.

She turns back to Bowen, and freezes. With his hand shaking, Bowen is pressing the gun against his own head, the one he snatched from the upload operator.

MAJOR

Hey... easy Bowen. What're you doing?

BOWEN

If I blow my brains out, you lose the key, right?

MAJOR

Hey c'mon... You're not gonna kill yourself... Right? You're Rhea's son. You'll have a bright future.

BOWEN

You let him and Loba go, and I'll surrender.

MAJOR

"Him"? You mean...
(pointing at Don)
Sure. Sure. Why not?
(to Don)
You can go. C'mon. Go.

Don steps back, his eyes saying, *so I can go?* The Major nods. Bowen nods too.

DON

(ashamed)

Sorry. But my daughter...

And he disappears in the night.

BOWEN

And Loba?

MAJOR

Don't worry. She'll be fine. Put the gun
down. I'll take you to her, okay? I swear.
You'll both be fine.

Yeh, right. The moment he puts the gun down, it's over.
Better to kill himself.

MAJOR

This could be a good thing, if you
think about it. When we get the
decryption key to the Remedy, we can
edit you. Make you forget a few things.
Unpleasant things. You'll be happy. Rich.

Bowen hesitates, not sure he has the balls to follow
through. Maybe there is another way out of this. He loosens
the gun from his temple.

MAJOR

And be with your *real* mom.

Bowen scowls, now fully determined to take his own life.

He jams the gun back against his head.

IN SLOW MOTION – Bowen shuts his eyes, accepting once again his brief life. He squeezes the trigger...

> SOLDIERS

NOOO!

CRACK! From behind, Don swings a heavy branch across SOLDIER #2's head, knocking him off balance. He wrestles for his rifle.

The Major and SOLDIER #1 turn to shoot him.

BOOM BOOM BOOM. Bowen gets them first.

Don rips the rifle free and fires into SOLDIER #2's neck, making him choke on his own blood.

Through the Major's helmet:

> AKIRA (V.O.)

Major, do you copy? Come in. Major?

Can you hear me?

Don taps DEACTIVATE ALL DRONES on the screen strapped to the Major's wrist and grabs her rifle. The drones drop from the sky, landing beside the bodies.

Bowen shoves the VR headset and tools into his backpack.

> BOWEN

Let's go.

They sprint off, Bowen's red headlamp marking the way through the trees until the light is swallowed by the dark.

The Major's fingers twitch.

EXT. CASTLE GARDEN - NIGHT

Akira stands alone by the large fountain, statues rising over a reflecting pool that mirrors the castle above.

>   AKIRA
>   (tapping her wrist with two
>   fingers)
>   Major, do you copy? Major?
>   (mouths)
>   Fuck.

EXT. FOREST - WATCH HUT - NIGHT

Bowen and Don enter a wooden wildlife-watching hut with a narrow rectangular window to observe animals. A red glow spills out from inside, casting an eerie hue across the surrounding dark.

INT. WATCH HUT - CONTINUOUS

The hut is poorly lit by Bowen's red headlamp. Don sits on a rough wooden bench, wiping sticky spiderwebs off his arms and face. He keeps watch through the narrow window, his body tense, rifle ready.

At the counter, Bowen resumes fixing the VR headset.

BOWEN
(showing the metallic disk)
You know, Don, this was revolutionary
once. It reads the brain. People used it
to control devices using their thoughts.
It's magi–

DON
(interrupting)
I know, man! You already told me. Don't
you remember?

Bowen looks confused, but keeps working. Don watches
him, worried, skeptical of Bowen's plan. And sanity.

Bowen adds the finishing touches and powers it on, red
neon lights firing up through the exposed chips.

DON

And? Does that piece of crap work?

Bowen pulls off his beanie and, having taken a deep breath, slides the headset over his eyes.

Chapter 14
Technology is alive

20 min read

Previously...

Bowen was being uploaded, but when **22%** of his consciousness was transferred, the operator was forced to halt the operation, as the upload device overheated. Bowen died on the table. To revive him, the operator injected a powerful drug that jolted him back to life.

Bowen and Don escaped to a hidden forest workshop to repair the damaged VR headset. After adding the finishing touches, Bowen powered it on.

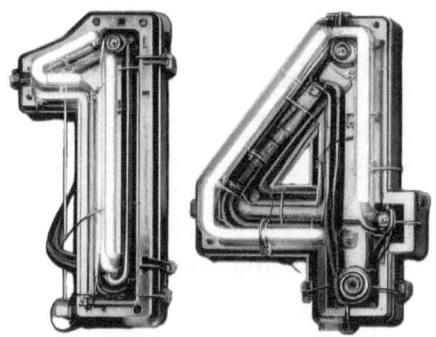

INT. CASTLE DUNGEON - NIGHT

FROM BOWEN'S POV (CRACKED IMAGE): He blinks, his vision is fractured. A web of black cracks overlays the dungeon, splitting the image where the physical-world lens is shattered. Through the shards, he sees hell. He is engulfed in flames, chained to the wall. Beside him, Loba hangs in the fire, burning alive.

Across the dungeon, the guard sits with his back turned, mesmerized by the screen on the wall. It broadcasts Rhea's Founding Day gala in the expansive gardens. To his right, the control display rests on the desk.

Bowen activates telekinesis, locking an ethereal blue

onto the control display. It shoots through the air toward him, slapping into his hand. He taps FIRE, and the flames vanish. Then he taps CHAINS, and the restraints dissolve.

Loba, paralyzed and roughed up, collapses. He catches her before she hits the floor, dropping the control display. As it clatters to the stone, the guard turns with eyes wide. He materializes a black rifle and opens fire.

Bowen shields Loba with his body, bullets slamming into his back. They do nothing to him. The guard frowns, baffled, and switches the gun mode from PARALYZE to KILL, his black rifle turning golden. He fires again. Bowen hunches lower, covering every inch of her. The lethal bullets are harmless to him, but he knows a single shot would kill her.

The guard stares at his weapon, inspecting it, trying to figure out what's wrong with it. Until it snaps out of his grip and into Bowen's waiting palm.

The man freezes, hands slowly rising in surrender. Bowen fights the exploding urge to pull the trigger right then and there. His hand shakes, fighting his own muscles. Instead, he reaches down with his free hand and sticks a device to Loba's neck. A message appears in midair.

Reactivating... 3%

On the broadcast, Rhea steps up to the podium on the castle terrace, overlooking the gardens, to give a speech.

Reactivating... 89%

Bowen keeps his aim on the monster, glaring at him. His finger tightens on the trigger. It would be so easy. One shot. He grinds his teeth, forcing himself to wait out the final seconds, glancing at the loading bar.

Reactivating... 100%

Loba's body unlocks. She springs up and charges the guard. With a powerful blow to his face, she knocks him down. Then, hands braced against the wall, she kicks him with all her strength, again and again and again.

Bowen lets her be. When she finally stops, her body shaking with adrenaline, he offers her the golden rifle. She takes it and shoots the guard nonstop, his body thrashing in violent seizures, until he stops moving.

Bowen wraps his arms around her from behind, but she pushes him away on reflex, breathing heavily, agitated, her golden-yellow eyes feral. She wants to fight. Kill. Cry.

> LOBA
>
> ...What? ...But how? Bullets didn't do anything to you.

> BOWEN
>
> I'm not using a lifepod. I'm using a very old device. One that can't send signals to the brain. So bullets can't do anything to me.

> LOBA

But... Where did you get a device like that?

> BOWEN

Listen. You need to go. Find a new server. Now.

> LOBA

What's the point? Once she passes the Act, I'll be dead anyway.

> BOWEN

I'll get her key. I'll get all the Tores, okay? Don't worry. Trust me.

He leans in to kiss her, but she drops her gaze. It hurts him, but he understands. She hasn't really come back to her body yet, and the fact that he felt it too only makes it worse.

INT. CASTLE BALLROOM - NIGHT

The opulent ballroom is empty, its polished hardwood shimmering under the glow of massive floating light-spheres. The ceiling rises so high it makes you feel insignificant. Tall vertical banners of the United Worlds drape the walls.

Above, on the mezzanine, an army of soldiers guards the terrace entrance, where Rhea stands behind a podium, overlooking the party below.

Bowen bursts in with the golden rifle and skids to a stop. The soldiers shoot him with their black paralyzer guns. Bowen just stands there, taking the bullets as if they were made of air.

The soldiers exchange troubled looks, then glance back at Rhea for orders. She steps in from the terrace, intrigued.

Bowen switches the selector mode on his weapon from KILL to PARALYZE, his golden rifle turning black, and opens fire. Soldiers drop by the dozens, paralyzed mid-motion, collapsing like marionettes with cut strings, some of them rolling down the stairs.

Rhea watches, impressed and entertained. Even a little proud. She carries the smirk of someone who feels untouchable.

The guests scream and run through the gardens in panic as gunfire echoes across the grounds.

More soldiers flood the room. Security personnel join too. They fire at Bowen from all directions, but he is unstoppable.

Until a soldier tackles him from behind, locking his arms. Another leaps on top, slamming a tracking device onto his neck. A message pops up.

Tracing...

More soldiers dive in, piling up like football players.

Suddenly, a black rifle wrapped in ethereal blue light bursts out of the pile. It spins in midair, firing nonstop into the dogpile. Bodies snap rigid, paralyzed.

Bowen erupts from underneath, shoving the frozen soldiers aside.

FROM BOWEN'S POV (CRACKED IMAGE): He paralyzes the last soldier standing, then rips the tracking device from his neck. He looks around. The polished hardwood is covered with frozen bodies.

He glares up at the mezzanine. Rhea stands there, her chin high and her arms open, utterly unafraid.

Bowen climbs the stairs, dodging paralyzed soldiers, each step heavy with the weight of everything she has taken from him.

At the top, they stand face to face, their matching green eyes locked.

> RHEA
>
> Son, I'm glad you're back. Akira told me
> what happened. You okay?

> BOWEN
>
> The key to your Tores. Hand it over.

She bursts into uncontrollable laughter. Bowen shoots her, but nothing happens, of course. He knew. She is just unbelievably annoying.

> RHEA
> (calming down)
> Sorry, son. But that's funny. So tell me,

why would I do that?

BOWEN

Those Tores belong to the people, so
they can govern themselves. That's what
you promised, remember?

RHEA

Oh, c'mon. I created the United Worlds.
You know how difficult that was? No
one can replicate the Worlds. Not
governments, not corporations, not
anyone. Even our top engineers don't
really understand the system anymore.

(chuckles)

It rewrote itself, Bowie. Don't you see?
This technology is alive.

(pause)

And you expect me to hand over control
of the miracle I brought into life? You
think that's fair?

BOWEN

And you think it's fair to the people who
came here believing they'd have a say on
how to live?

RHEA
(scoffs, shakes her head)
Look, you have no idea how many times
(with disdain)
"the people" voted for laws that would've been catastrophic for our country. Absolute disasters.
(clicks tongue, *no no no*)
They can't be trusted to make good decisions. Especially not in groups. You know, what the majority wants isn't always what's right. And hey, I'm not saying I ignore their votes, okay?

A new troop of soldiers rushes in, stepping around the paralyzed bodies. Rhea dismisses them with a flick of her hand.

RHEA
I don't ignore their votes. I study them. What they want. What they propose. I take it into account. But I'm not gonna let 'em ruin it. Ruin what I've built with so much sacrifice. Seriously, trust me. I know what's best for our country, okay?

BOWEN
Oh yeh, like spying on people, right? Yeh,

nah, sure. That's a good thing. People
love having no privacy at all.

RHEA

Sweetie, you're too young, so you might
not understand now. But you know what
your daddy used to say?

Bowen is taken aback by the mention of his father, a man
he never knew, and never will.

RHEA

"For the beauty of the rose, we also water
the thorns." Without the thorns, the rose
gets eaten. Thorns are necessary for
survival, see?

BOWEN

What the fuck are you saying?

RHEA

(sighs)

I'm saying, Bowen, that sometimes, you
have to do things people think are wrong.
So people see the thorns as something
dangerous, right? But thorns protect the
rose. See what I'm saying? Spying is just
the necessary price to protect those we
love.

His frown deepens.

> RHEA

> Look, you weren't here when the Worlds
> started, okay? So you don't know how
> dangerous it was. Möbius? You don't
> know them like I do. I'm sure you don't
> because, if you did, you wouldn't be
> hanging out with them. That parasite
> Loba?
>> (scoffs)
> Oh. She's the worst. I have stories about
> her that would freeze your blood. And
> they're using you, Bowie. Don't you see?
> They want chaos to control our beautiful
> country. A country so special that it has
> the power to access minds. You want *that*
> power to fall under the wrong hands?

> BOWEN

> It already has, you delusional, egomaniac
> bitch.

> RHEA

> Hey. Careful. We'll correct that behavior
> when we edit you.

BOWEN

Good thing you don't have the Remedy
anymore.

RHEA

Mhm, but that's about to change. You
know J.S., right? The Möbius guy with
four arms? Well, he has the decryption
key. And he's willing to trade.

BOWEN
(chuckles)
Bullshit. He'd never. You're even dumber
than I thought.

RHEA

Hey, c'mon. Don't be like that. My
plan was always to raise you as my kid,
and future heir of all this. I'm so sorry
for everything that happened to you.
Honestly.

She puts her hand on his shoulder and smiles.

RHEA

Look, hear me out, okay? Let me... Let
me upload you so I can recover what's
mine. And I promise I'll take care of you.
I promise. The Human Preservation Act?

It won't affect you. You'll be exempt, of
course.

(caressing his face)

You know, it's time you join our family.

What do you say, Bowie?

He takes her hand, forcing a smile. She smiles back.
Looks like he is falling for her proposal. At least, that's the
impression he wants to give. Without a word, he locks a blue
ethereal target onto her and lifts her off the ground.

RHEA
(to herself)

Command: telek

Nothing happens. Her eyes widen.

RHEA
(louder, to herself)

Command: ghost.

Nothing.

RHEA
(to herself)

Command: vanish!

Again. Nothing. She can't use any powers while being
locked by someone's telekinesis. For the first time, Rhea is
powerless.

Bowen shows her the syringe filled with glowing yellow

liquid, the one he stole from Dr Holland's lab. Her face crumbles in fear. Genuine, mortal fear.

He glides forward, pushing Rhea through the air toward the open terrace doors. They drift out into the night air under the full moon, its reflection rippling across the ocean, the water glittering with starlight.

He pulls her closer, inches away.

> BOWEN
> (pressing the syringe to her
> jugular)
> You never configured defenses for this,
> did you?

> RHEA
> Bowen! I'm your mother!

> BOWEN
> Abi is my real mom.

> RHEA
> I'm your biological mother!

> BOWEN
> Yeh, you know what? Sometimes...
> artificial can be more real than biological.
> (puts his thumb over the plunger)
> Okay, Rhea, look. Don't test me. Just give
> me the Tores, and I'll let you live. 'Kay?

That's all I want.

She looks away, calculating. He presses the syringe harder. He means it. She grimaces, then exhales violently and nods, defeated.

A golden key materializes in the air before them.

BOWEN
Is this really the key?

RHEA
The vault sent the key back to me when
you broke in. Go ahead, check it yourself.
It's all there. I don't lie. I never do.

BOWEN
Show me.

Rhea swipes two fingers across the key. A screen materializes showing 1.3 billion Tores. Bowen grins.

But the grin turns into a scowl when he sees Akira running toward them. He snatches the key and stuffs it inside his jacket.

General Akira removes her helmet.

Bowen swallows, feeling sorry for her. Her mother is still in there, in some weird, fucked-up way.

RHEA
Akira, if he doesn't give me the key
back... kill yourself.

Akira glares at her, stunned. Rhea shoots her a commanding look, her eyes saying, *you'd better do it.*

Akira slowly raises the handgun to her own head. Bowen grabs Rhea's neck, hard.

> RHEA
>
> Let me go. And give me back my key.
> (pause)
> You're hurting my neck, son.

Bowen doesn't loosen his grip.

> RHEA
>
> Okay. Enough. I'll give you 10 seconds to release me and hand my key back. If you don't, she will kill herself.

Bowen stares at Akira. At his mom.

> RHEA
>
> 10... 9... 8...

> BOWEN
>
> ...That's not her anymore.

> RHEA
>
> But she can be. You know, you can get her back. Back to who she was before we changed her.
> (off his skeptical *Tsk*)
> I'm telling you the truth. The Remedy

has a reverse feature. It will rewire the
brain back to how it was.

BOWEN

Your program works like shit. She'll die
if I try that.

RHEA

Yeah, maybe. But maybe not. She was
the one who survived the operation
after all, remember? Probably has a good
chance of surviving it again.
(pause)
Wouldn't you like to get her back?

She smirks, noticing Bowen is getting convinced.

RHEA

Where was I? 7? 7... 6... 5...

What if she's telling the truth? What if he can get his
mom back? She's in there somewhere. He knows she's in
there somewhere.

He looks at the gun pressed against Abi's temple. He is
fast, but he can't stop a trigger pull. If he attacks, she dies. But
if he leaves... If he finds the decryption key to the Remedy
himself... Maybe he can save her. Maybe she can be herself
again. Maybe they can be together again after all.

RHEA

3... 2... 1...

Bowen shoves Rhea backward, throws the key at her, and launches into the sky, flying away.

INT. WATCH HUT - NIGHT

Bowen pulls off the VR headset, his face flushed with frustration. He staggers back, breath trembling.

DON

What happened? Is Loba okay?

BOWEN

She's fine.

(exhales violently)

Fuck!

Bowen kicks the wooden counter, making the tools fall to the ground. He paces in a tight circle, hands on his head, gripping his messy hair.

DON

Bo, what happened?

BOWEN

I don't have Rhea's key. And now she'll pass the Human Preservation Act.

(voice breaks)

I had it. I had the fucking key

(slapping his own forehead)

and I gave it back to her. Fuck!

He crouches, hands on his knees, having difficulty breathing.

BOWEN

Jesus. What the fuck did I do, Don?

(pause)

Loba... 99 million people... they're dead

now 'cause of me.

He collapses onto the bench, elbows on knees, nails digging into his scalp, mind racing 300 miles per hour.

Slowly, his grip loosens. He lowers his hands.

BOWEN

Don... there's one more thing I gotta do.

(looks up, haunted)

And I'll need your help.

Don closes his eyes, hesitates, wanting to say no, but he exhales and nods, surrendering to whatever comes next.

EXT. DIRT MOUNTAIN ROAD - DAWN

Bowen and Don race down the dirt mountain road on the rusty green bike, Don balancing on the back rack, gripping Bowen's shoulders.

Far below, the lake lies still, reflecting the deep purple sky. The horizon burns with a thin line of orange fire. The silhouettes of trees and mountains cut sharp against the rising light.

They reach the shore and jump into the same blue fishing boat the soldiers stole earlier. They rip across the glass-smooth water at max speed.

INT. SCRAP WAREHOUSE - DAWN

Homeless people and addicts have taken over the place. They're everywhere.

Bowen and Don enter, rifles in hand, moving cautiously through the cluttered aisles, avoiding eye contact as they push toward the back.

INT. WAREHOUSE BASEMENT - CONTINUOUS

Bowen reaches into his backpack and pulls out the VR headset, handing it to Don.

BOWEN
Take good care of it.

DON
(clasps Bowen's hand)
Hey. You sure about this? 'Cause, you know, after this, you won't be able to leave the Worlds. Ever. You know that, right?

Bowen nods, then leans down and slaps the operator's

face to wake him up.

> UPLOAD OPERATOR
>
> Wha–?
>
> (wiping drool)
>
> ...Don't want any trouble. Please.

> BOWEN
>
> Upload me.

The operator stares, bewildered. Don kicks his boot.

> DON
>
> Go on. You heard him.

> UPLOAD OPERATOR
>
> (struggling to stand)
>
> N-no, I-I-I'll do it if you want to. But you gotta understand, kid. Resuming an upload after it was interrupted...? You don't want that. It's 20 times more dangerous. I'm not exaggerating, okay? People die. It's not safe.
>
> (grabbing his head)
>
> And hey, you know what? I'm not feeling too well. My head... The drugs... I-I-I can't.

> BOWEN
>
> (to Don)

If something goes wrong...
> (glares at the operator)

kill him.

The old man freezes, his mouth hanging open. Don worries Bowen isn't thinking straight – he looks like a maniac – but he still motions for the operator to move.

The operator checks the upload device and turns in panic.

> UPLOAD OPERATOR
>
> Where is it? You have it, right?

> BOWEN
>
> What now?

> UPLOAD OPERATOR
>
> The memory. C'mon. The partial upload data.
>
> (off Bowen's clueless face)
>
> Kid, 22% of you was uploaded, but the memory isn't here anymore. So you don't have it?
>
> (Bowen shakes his head)
>
> Oh boy. Someone took it then. This adds even more risk. You shouldn't do this.

> BOWEN
>
> ...You're saying someone has 22% of me?

UPLOAD OPERATOR

...Correct, but you're missing the point.
The point is, the operation's even riskier
now. It was already dangerous, and now
it's worse.
(to Don)
I don't think he's in any condition to
make important decisions like this.

DON
(to Bowen)
What if the key was in that 22%?

Bowen lies back on the round table, hoping for the best.

BOWEN
I'm ready.

The operator is baffled and astonished by the kid's
stubbornness. He glances at Don to see if he'll intervene,
but Don motions to begin.

UPLOAD OPERATOR
Okay. Fine. But if we do this, we can't
do it here. The machine might overheat
again.

Bowen sits upright, thinking.

INT. WAREHOUSE - CONTINUOUS

Bowen shoves the operator forward, keeping him in view in case he tries to escape. Behind them, the humanoid military robot follows, its stomp heavy and mechanical. It clutches the heavy transport case to its chest, its helmet and armor still fouled with vomit. Don covers the rear, his eyes sweeping the aisles to make sure nothing gets near them.

> DON
> (eyeing the robot)
> You sure that thing won't turn on us?

> BOWEN
> You mean the robot? Don't worry.
> Reprogramming this stuff is easy.

Don lifts his eyebrows. *Yeah, easy for you.*

They step outside into the gray morning light and move down the sidewalk, dodging the filthy tents and piles of trash.

At the lakeside, Bowen and Don step into the blue fishing boat and take the transport case from the robot. The old man climbs in last, shaking from the cold, and from fear.

EXT. BOAT - MORNING

They navigate close along the lakeshore and turn sharply into a narrow break in the reeds.

At a hidden bay swallowed by trees, Bowen flips a switch,

dropping the anchor. He lies on the deck, arms folded over his chest like a man settling into a coffin. His whole body is tight, bracing for what's coming.

The operator fits the device around Bowen's head, and injects him with anesthesia. As Bowen drifts into unconsciousness, the operator makes a few adjustments, then taps START.

Inside Bowen's brain, beams of searing energy thread through his neurons, forcing them to flare into violent flashes, tearing the connections apart as they die. Networks decay, turning from gold to black.

Blood spills from Bowen's nose.

On the monitor, virtual neurons form, rebuilding his brain.

Uploading consciousness... 35%

A 3D brain forms in real-time, pink and purple and red neurons branching out into a chaotic web.

Blood leaks from his ears, pooling on the white fiberglass deck.

Don holds Bowen's hand.

Uploading consciousness... 57%

The veins in Bowen's neck and temples surge to the surface, a network under too much pressure, fighting to hold. His biological brain is dying.

An alarm goes off. DANGER flashes on the screen.

The operator rushes to adjust the settings on the control panels, lowering one bar, raising another, sliding a dial, tapping glowing tags that appear as suggestions, flipping switches on and off...

Blood bursts out of Bowen's eyes, dark and unrelenting.

The blue fishing boat rests on the lake, the water reflecting the fiery reds and golds of the autumn forest.

The IMAGE ROTATES 90 DEGREES, the world turning sideways, as a TIMELAPSE unfolds. Clouds race, shadows stretch, the sky deepens in color. Though the sun travels across the sky, the rotating image locks it in place.

By the time the rotation settles, the line between the forest and the mirrored lake runs vertically through the image, creating a surreal, disorienting view of nature.

The flatline stretches into a piercing *BEEEEEEEEP*.

A pool of blood spreads across the deck around Bowen's head. It looks like something exploded inside his skull.

EXT. LOBA'S TREEHOUSE - PORCH - DUSK

High atop the tallest tree in the lush jungle, the sky burns with colorful clouds. Loba clutches her head, leaning against the handrail of her bohemian porch.

Bowen materializes at the far end of the deck.

They freeze, staring at each other. They've been through so much.

He shows her the decagon badge on his shoulder and

shrugs. *It's all right.*

They walk toward each other, cicadas singing in the warm jungle air, the massive waterfalls roaring up the mist-shrouded cliffs.

As he steps closer, the light catches his face. His eyes are no longer green. They are purple.

> LOBA
>
> Your eyes. You changed them.
>
> (he nods)
>
> Why?

> BOWEN
>
> Don't you like it?

She wrinkles her nose, shaking her head. His purple eyes seem to plead, *c'mon, don't be mean.* She tries to hold the frown, but a smile breaks through anyway. He takes her hand and smiles back.

Chapter 15
The self must belong to itself

13 min read

Previously...

Bowen confronted Rhea and managed to take the key with her Tores, but was forced to surrender it when Rhea ordered General Akira, Bowen's mind-controlled mother, to hold a gun to her own head. Rhea revealed the Remedy has a reverse feature, offering a slim chance to restore Abi's mind.

Desperate to stop the Human Preservation Act, Bowen decided to upload himself to access the Mystery Key encoded in his brain. But there was a problem: the data from his failed first upload was missing. Facing the terrifying possibility the key might be inside the missing fragment, Bowen uploaded anyway.

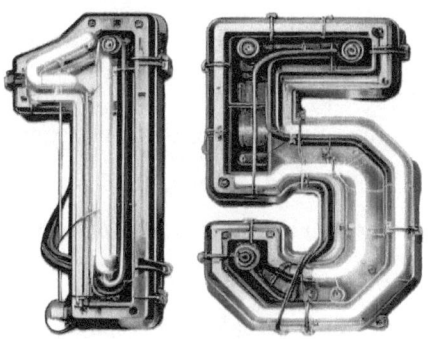

INT. MÖBIUS OPS CENTER - NIGHT

Loba hands Bowen a purple potion.

BOWEN

This won't fuck me up, right?

Loba smiles and presses the potion to his face until he drinks it.

Loba's fingers dance across the keyboard, elegant, like she's playing the piano, her nails clacking in rhythm.

As she taps ENTER, screens materialize in midair, forming a half-circle arc around her, each one showing a different version of what Bowen sees. Together, they display all the layers of his vision.

LOBA

Okay now. Look around.

As Bowen obeys, the screens react instantly. On the first screen, the outline layer redraws itself into thin black-and-white contour lines, like a sketch of the room with no fill, just edges. On the second, the shape layer rearranges into soft, abstract forms. On the third, the color layer washes and rewashes itself to match the hangar's palette. On the fourth, the motion layer updates streaks every time he shifts his view.

LOBA

You're sure it's in the visual cortex, right?

BOWEN

I don't know. That's what Rhea said. That's why I can't see colors – couldn't see colors in the Offline.

DON

Or maybe it's not there. You know, 22% of Bowen got uploaded before. The key could be there.

VAISHNAVI

And where is that 22%?

BOWEN

We don't know. But it doesn't matter. It's

there. You'll see.

LOBA

'Kay. Keep looking around.

(pause)

Slower. Don't move too fast.

The images on the screens morph like living paintings as he moves, responding to every shift of his attention.

But some tiny fragments stay exactly the same.

LOBA

Good. Keep going.

Bowen sweeps the hangar.

He turns and stares at Loba. Her golden-yellow eyes burning bright against her darker skin, her thick lips, the wild crown of her long black curls. It is the kind of beauty that makes you want to pin a floating image to your field of view, just so you can take it everywhere you go.

Loba ignores the look, focused on the data. She pulls the tiny fragments that refuse to move, her hands guiding them like a conductor leading an orchestra.

Loba snaps her fingers, freezing the feed. The screens stop updating what Bowen sees. She draws the tiny glowing fragments together with slow gestures, fusing them into a code.

Loba types it in, hits ENTER, and a purple message appears on every screen.

3.96 BILLION TORES

Silence. They let it sink in. They did it. They took away Rhea's power. She and her secret Council no longer have the majority. And most importantly, Rhea won't be able to pass the Human Preservation Act.

The four of them laugh and shout and jump and kick, feeling the crushing pressure lift off their shoulders. They come together in a blissful hug. Loba howls, released from her haunting past, wiping the tears from her wolf eyes.

> DON
> The transfer script is ready to run whenever you say.

> BOWEN
> Included uploads, right?

> DON
> (nods)
> Each upload will get seven Tores. Bio citizens get six, since they already hold one. So at the end of the day, everyone will have seven. It doesn't matter if they're biological or artificial.

They wrap their arms around each other and stare at the TRANSFER button, its lights rippling away from it like water. Their hands move to push it.

BOWEN

Wait.

Bowen bites his lip, searching for how to say it.

DON

What?

BOWEN

Nothing. Nothing. Let's do it.

LOBA

What's wrong?

BOWEN

No, nothing. It's just that... I was thinking maybe we can, you know, use the Tores before transferring them. To kill the Human Preservation Act, right? And then we transfer all of it when the voting closes.

Bowen frowns and looks down, embarrassed for suggesting this. He glances at them to see their reactions.

LOBA

But we can't do that. We can't be that hypocritical. I mean...

(pause)

Right?

They're considering it. They know what's at risk, but they also know it goes against what they've been fighting for.

> BOWEN
>
> Forget it. Forget I even mentioned it, okay? Let's do this.

> DON
>
> No, hold on. Let's think about it.

> LOBA
>
> We can't. If we do this, we become her.

> BOWEN
>
> Become Rhea? C'mon... Using the Tores once to stop a mass murder isn't the same as ruling with them forever, don't you agree?

> LOBA
> (sighs)
> I don't know. We said their votes should matter, so let their votes matter.

> BOWEN
>
> But a vote that decides whether a minority should live or die? That's not democracy.

DON

This vote should've never been allowed.
Don't we have laws that protect people's
rights?

LOBA

We do have laws that protect people's
rights. Laws that protect *biological*
people's rights.
(pause)
Look at the name she used, for fuck's
sake. Human Preservation Act. As if we
aren't human.

Bowen scratches his neck, sick at the thought of sharing
Rhea's genes. And uneasy knowing he once thought like her.

BOWEN

If we let the people vote on it, aren't we,
in some way, legitimizing extermination
as a valid option?

VAISHNAVI

Look, I hate to say it, but if people truly
support the Human Preservation Act,
which, by the way, only a handful of
hardcore purists do, if they truly want to
pass it, it'll come back anyway. They can

submit it again shortly after.

(pause)

And lemme tell you something else. If we use the Tores to kill this Act and then a similar Act is proposed again...

LOBA

The public will see it as proof that uploads can't be trusted, and more people will turn against us.

VAISHNAVI

Exactly. Can you imagine the backlash? It's gonna be worse. Much worse.

LOBA

Yeah, I agree. And look. There's hate against uploads. Trust me, I know that very well. But enough hate to kill 99 million? I don't think so.

BOWEN

So we transfer them. We transfer the Tores now.

Loba nods. Everyone nods too. They have to do this. Do it the right way. Together, they reach out and tap the TRANSFER button.

Transferring...

On the big screen, the pie chart showing the voting power distribution changes. The largest slice with the MYSTERY KEY tag shrinks, while the smallest slice labeled THE PEOPLE slowly consumes the rest.

Transfer complete

The people now have 70% of all Tores.

EXT. DESERT TERRACE - DAY

An oasis-like terrace carved from smooth sandstone, all curves and arches, looks out onto a warm horizon of dunes and distant cliffs. A young man with a decagon badge on his shoulder rests on a comfy round couch, reading.

A notification appears in midair.

You received 7 Tores and a necklace
from Möbius.

VIEW DETAILS   DISMISS

He frowns, puzzled.

INT. CINEMA - DAY

A group of friends watches a movie inside an IMAX-size, 360-degree screen in an empty auditorium.

Notifications pop up silently for all of them.

You received 6 Tores and a necklace

A symphony of looks that say, *what the hell?*

EXT. DESERTED PARADISE BEACH - DAY

A teenage girl surfs a perfect endless wave while two families grill BBQ on the shore of a white-sand beach. The sun shines in a cloudless sky.

The adults talk and laugh, until they get notifications that silence them.

> You received 6 Tores and a necklace
> from Möbius.

They exchange skeptical looks.

EXT. LOBA'S JUNGLE - DUSK

Loba and Bowen struggle to stay upright on a square wooden raft, laughing as the rushing river tosses them side to side. A deep roar builds ahead. Louder.

IN SLOW MOTION – The river ends, and they fall over the edge of a 300-foot waterfall, a drop as steep as a skyscraper, holding hands, wide-eyed.

They shout with pure thrill. And disappear into the mist.

They burst from the fog, flying up into the jungle sky, their hair blowing in the wind. They race toward the clouds, neck to neck. She leads. He overtakes. Then she leads again.

Above the clouds, there is complete silence. A deserted

heaven under a deep purple twilight. Peace is interrupted as they burst through the cloud floor, spinning together.

They dive hand in hand, arms stretched wide, embracing the wind.

They fly close to the massive series of waterfalls, dancing in the mist, getting wet, teasing each other.

Behind the cascading walls of water, plunging with rhythmic sound, they stand forehead to forehead, soaked, breathing heavily. Adrenaline runs through their bodies.

Their eyes carry something no words can hold. Something no one else could understand. Their bond was forged in admiration, laughter, music... and trauma.

> BOWEN
> (deep breath, smiles)
> The air is so fresh.

She takes his arm, the one with the decagon badge on it.

> LOBA
> I'll take it off.

> BOWEN
> (shakes his head)
> It's okay. Kinda like it, actually.
> (takes her hand)
> But I want the Möbius tattoo.

She tames her smile, though her twitching wolf ears

betray her. His fingers brush the soft black fur, petting them gently. She bites her lip, embarrassed but leaning into the touch.

She takes off his shirt and inks the tattoo onto his chest. His gaze lights with devotion, a warmth she feels immediately. With a soft smile, she turns his face away.

EXT. LOBA'S TREEHOUSE - PORCH - DAWN

The sun rises over the falls, casting gold and rose across the water.

Loba and Bowen lie naked in a hammock bed, eyes shut, listening to the jungle wake up. Zen smiles linger after a night of passion. Her fingers trace his chest, over the newly inked Möbius strip.

Along the handrail, black ants carry a heavy twig – when a blue manakin with black wings and a cherry-red crown flies past and snatches it.

Bowen gets a notification.

> DON sent you a message.

INT. MÖBIUS OPS CENTER - MORNING

Loba and Bowen materialize in the hangar doorway, looking rested and glowing. Post-best-sex-ever energy.

> LOBA
> Wow, what's going on?

Don and V argue in heated bursts near the main console. He shoots V a challenging look, a nod that says, *go ahead, tell them.*

> VAISHNAVI
>
> It's J.S. He's still missing. And I don't know what he'll do. You know, he has the decryption key to the Remedy.

> DON
> (to Bowen)
>
> V wants to use the logic bomb. The one you planted in Rhea's program.

> BOWEN
>
> Wait. What? You want to destroy the Remedy? No. No fucking way. It's my only chance to get my mom back.

> VAISHNAVI
>
> Look, you don't know him like Loba and I do, okay? He's been ignoring our messages since the ambush. I messaged him again, told him everything we did, what you did, and still nothing. Don't know what he'll do.
> (to Loba)
> Loba, c'mon. Don't you think it's weird?

Disappearing like that?

BOWEN
So he's not responding?
(to Loba)
Not even to you?

Loba shakes her head. Bowen looks away, biting his lip, hands laced over his head.

DON
Can't we first try to find out what he's planning to do with it? Loba, you must know someone.

LOBA
I can ask around.

VAISHNAVI
Seriously? We don't have time for that. It might already be too late.

Bowen murmurs something under his breath, almost hoping no one heard.

LOBA
What's that?

He hesitates, debating whether saying this out loud will corner him into an unwinnable argument.

LOBA

What is it?

BOWEN

Rhea said something... I thought she was lying or just being dumb. 'Cause if J.S. was negotiating with her to trade the key to the Remedy, he was clearly manipulating her. He isn't gonna actually give *her* the key. Right?

V and Loba lock eyes. This is more serious than they thought.

BOWEN

You're saying he would?

All eyes on Bowen as his thoughts begin to spiral. He paces a few steps, rubbing his face, fully aware of what they're thinking.

BOWEN

No, no. I-I can't. You don't understand. I thought I'd lost her forever. If I destroy the Remedy, it's like... killing her myself.

A long, heavy silence fills the hangar.

DON

Bo... if he's negotiating with Rhea, you're not getting the key anyway.

Bowen freezes. That hits him. His eyes dart left to right, searching desperately for another way out.

There isn't. He knows that's true. And his mother would want him to protect people from this.

Bowen's shoulders slowly collapse, and his brow loosens, the fight draining out of him as the truth settles in.

Defeated, Bowen walks toward his workstation, where he types a command and hits ENTER. The keyboard transforms into a pulsing red microphone icon.

> BOWEN
>
> I have to say a phrase. Once I say it, the
> logic bomb will go off.

Loba puts an encouraging hand on his shoulder.

He presses the microphone icon, and an audio waveform appears across the screen, pulsing with each breath he takes.

> BOWEN
>
> The self...
> > (pause)
> must belong...
> > (pause)
> to its—

A whooshing sound at the hangar doorway makes everyone turn and pull out their golden guns.

J.S. strides in with his jaw tight, his four arms swing at his sides, heading straight toward Bowen.

LOBA

Oh shit. Look who's back. Where were
you?

J.S. stops inches from Bowen, glaring with his intense
black eyes. Bowen shoots Loba a quick look. *What the fuck?*

J.S.
(to Bowen)
All my friends are dead because of you.

J.S. shakes his head and exhales violently, then extends
his primary right hand to Bowen.

J.S.
But you did good afterwards.

BOWEN
(shakes his hand)
I'm really sorry about your friends. Truly.
I'll carry that with me, always.

VAISHNAVI
(to J.S.)
Is it true? You're negotiating with Rhea?
Are you outta your fucking mind? Tell
me you didn't give her the decryption
key to the Remedy. Please, tell me you
didn't.

J.S. reaches into his pocket with a lower hand and pulls

out the decryption key.

> BOWEN
>
> Can I have it?

> J.S.
>
> Yeah, but look, Rhea and her Council
> aren't in the system. That was the first
> thing I checked.

> BOWEN
>
> It's for someone else.

Bowen slots the key into the console, logging into the Remedy. The interface flashes green: ACCESS GRANTED.

> DON
>
> "The self belongs..." What was the
> phrase?

> BOWEN
>
> The self must belong to itself.

Bowen types AKIRA SAKAI and hits ENTER.

> Searching...

And there she is. He taps her name and an image of her avatar appears. Next to it is a control panel with a REVERSE button.

Bowen swallows hard. This could save her.

Or kill her.

Loba wraps her arms around him from behind, pressing her cheek against his. He breathes in her scent, loving it.

Bowen taps REVERSE and a progress tracker appears.

Reversing... 1%

Bowen glances back at the others, worried. *Will this work?*

Chapter 16
Tell me that's not a soul

15 min read

Previously...

Loba found the Mystery Key inside Bowen's brain, and together they transferred the Tores to the people, both biological and artificial. For the first time in United Worlds history, everyone's vote will count.

Bowen then used the Remedy to reverse the rewiring done to his mother. The process could save her or kill her. They will find out soon.

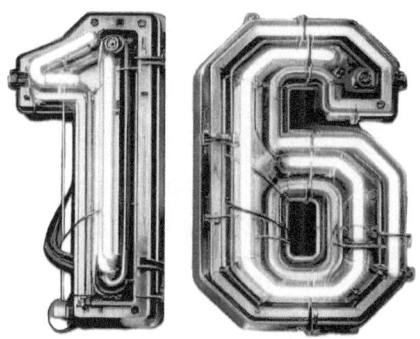

INT. COUNCIL CHAMBERS - DAY

The Council gathers on a circular marble island rising from a milky turquoise lake. Floor-to-ceiling glass walls frame a massive blue glacier and snow-capped mountains, turning the room into a temple of ice and light.

At the center of the arched marble table, Rhea sits dressed in her signature black. General Akira occupies the far right seat. In the open space before them, the U.W. insignia is engraved into the polished floor.

Shocked and worried, they watch a giant vertical floating screen where a beautiful young INFLUENCER with wolf ears is broadcasting live to more than 30 million viewers.

She gestures constantly, her long nails painted in a flurry
of different colors, matching her eyes that flash the same
vibrant spectrum.

> INFLUENCER
>
> I-I-I... I still can't believe it. I mean... I'm
> gonna be honest. I always thought what
> Loba said was, you know, a conspiracy
> theory. Who didn't, right?
>
> (chuckles)
>
> But turns out, it's not! She was right.
> Möbius was right.
>
> (leans in)
>
> And if they were right about the Tores...
> don't you think they might be right about
> everything else too?

One of the Council members faints with his eyes open,
his face hitting the marble table with a dull thud.

> INFLUENCER
>
> Rhea told us uploads were a threat. But
> she was the real threat.

On her livestream, the WANTED posters of Loba,
Bowen, Don, V, and J.S. appear around her, their meaning
unmistakably reversed.

> INFLUENCER
>
> Look. You know me. I believed uploads

weren't human, that they had no souls.
But after what Möbius did? Uploads
fighting for our freedom? After the way
we treated them?
(pause)
Loba and Möbius risked everything for
people who hated them.

One by one, Council members faint as their connections
are cut. Panic erupts. They shove each other, scrambling
toward the narrow marble catwalk, racing for the swirling
exit portal framed by a stone archway. Some try to fly, lifting
off into the air, but mid-flight their connection is cut and they
collapse like marionettes with cut strings, splashing into the
freezing turquoise water.

Others go limp mid-stride, toppling off the bridge. Bodies
pile up on the stone like soulless shells.

INFLUENCER
They could have kept the Tores for
themselves, but they gave them to the
people. They exposed the truth. It's the
most democratic act in United Worlds
history. It's the most *humane* act in
United Worlds history.

Rhea stands frozen, paralyzed by a terror she never
believed possible. She glares at Akira, who remains seated,

completely calm. The General wears a small, victorious smirk.

INFLUENCER

Uploads aren't replacing humanity. They *are* humanity.

(pause)

Now that we, the people, have the majority of Tores, the power is finally ours. Let our first real vote as United Worlds citizens be against genocide. I urge you, all of you, to vote NO on the Human Preservation Act. Stand with Loba. Stand with uploads. Stand with what it truly means to be human.

(puts the Möbius necklace on)

Thank you to everyone at Möbius for your service to this nation.

The influencer lifts the Möbius necklace toward the camera, so close that it fills the entire screen.

QUICK SHOT of a wall of monitors tracking people's intimate moments, many of them putting on their Möbius necklaces. As they do, each screen goes dead, replaced by the same message: TRACKING ERROR.

Desperate, Rhea scrambles over the marble table, abandoning all dignity. She sprints toward the catwalk, but her legs give out. She collapses hard onto the floor, her soulless body landing directly across the U.W. insignia.

The floating screen shifts from the influencer's stream to the news, its lower third reading, "BREAKING NEWS: RHEA AND INDUSTRY TITANS HAVE BEEN ARRESTED."

INT. MOUNTAIN CABIN - DUSK

A futuristic, stylish wooden lodge glows with the light of a fireplace. Expansive windows overlook a heavy snowfall, the setting sun bathing the snow-covered mountains in soft purples and pinks.

Abi materializes in the center of the room, wearing her U.W. Army uniform. Her long gray hair spills loose to her waist.

Bowen runs to her and pulls her into a hug. She chokes back tears, until she breaks, sobbing. Devastated. He cries with her.

ABI

God, I missed you so much.

BOWEN

I missed you too, Mom.

They hold each other. It feels like a dream. He got her back from the dead. And from worse.

He leads her into a bedroom where panoramic glass walls reveal nothing but endless, snow-laden pine trees. A smaller fireplace glows softly in the corner.

BOWEN

Looks like Homewood, doesn't it?

(whispering to himself)

But with luxuries.

(inhales deeply)

Pine trees. You smell it? Just like home,

right?

He waits for her face to light up. Instead, she gives a tight-lipped smile and sighs, looking up at the skylight half-covered in snow. His excitement drains, sensing her distance. Trying to recover, he adds quickly...

BOWEN

Lemme know if it's too much snow, okay? I can show you how to control the weather.

She is drawn to a wall covered in photos of her and Bowen through the years. Hikes. Birthdays. Gardening. Picnics at the lake. She winces, missing that life. Bowen catches her reaction and his smile fades, realizing she will need time to adjust.

BOWEN

Okay. Lemme know if you need anything.

I'll let you... Yeh.

He gives her an awkward hug and leaves her to settle.

Alone, Abi catches her reflection in the glass of a framed

photo. The Army insignia glares back.

She rips off the uniform as if it were burning her skin, and throws it into the fireplace. The flames crackle, consuming the fabric into ash. She stares into the fire, her mind lost somewhere far beyond.

* * *

They sit at a wooden table overflowing with a beautifully arranged feast: prime rib with herb crust, grilled lobster, truffle mashed potatoes, wild mushroom risotto, roasted vegetables with balsamic glaze, a plate of cheeses and fruit.

Abi prays with her eyes shut, her face tightening with torment. She makes the sign of the cross, but her eyes stay closed, dreading the moment she has to open them and accept this new reality.

She sighs and finally opens her eyes, glaring at the food with deep irritation. Bowen smiles and takes her hand. But she pulls it away.

                    BOWEN
            Mom... you okay?

She frowns and scoffs.

                    BOWEN
            What? Talk to me. I know this is –

                    ABI
                (interrupting)

I died, Bowen.

(pause)

And now what? I'm... *this*? What is this?

She stares at her hands like they belong to someone else.

ABI

I didn't want this. This isn't me anymore.
I'm dead, don't you get it? I didn't want
this.

She rubs her arms, as if trying to scrub off this virtual
skin.

BOWEN

But... aren't you happy we're together
again?

A tear rolls down her cheek. He stands up and hugs her
from behind.

BOWEN

Mom, it's okay. It will get better.

ABI

(shaking her head)

I... This place...

(sighs)

There are just too many memories. I
was a completely different person in the
United Worlds. I was horrible, Bowie.

(covers her face)

Oh God.

BOWEN

(uncovers her face)

Hey. C'mon. Don't be too tough on yourself. I'm sure you're exaggerating. I mean, you saved me. You rescued me from the lab.

She looks at him, drowning with guilt.

BOWEN

...What?

ABI

Uh, well... I "rescued" you because, uh... I wanted the Tores for myself.

(he pulls away)

I'm sorry. I told you. I was horrible. Franklin, your biological father, knew Rhea was plotting against him. He ordered me to hide the key inside your brain. I ran 'cause she was going to kill me next. And I took you so she wouldn't get the Tores.

(looking down)

My plan... was to wait until you turned

21... and upload you.

Bowen reels back, stung. He sinks into his chair.

BOWEN

It's okay. You're not that person anymore, you hear me? You're not. You're nothing like that. You took good care of me. Always.

ABI

Not always. At the beginning? I was a... mess. You don't know, Bowie. Imagine going from being the General, leading the Worlds' Army, working with the most powerful people in the world... To hiding in a hippie community.

(scoffs)

I hated Homewood. Truly. Hated everyone there. And I hated myself the most. For being stuck there, raising...

(stops herself)

And you don't know how paranoid I was, okay? And... well, things got outta control.

INT. BOWEN'S HOUSE - DAY - FLASHBACK

The cramped main room is dark. Only a few rays of

sunlight filter through the drapes.

Abi is passed out cold on the couch with a whiskey bottle loosely gripped in her hand. 5-year-old Bowen tries to wake her. He is burning up, sweat soaking through his clothes. His small hands tremble as he shakes his mother, but she is too drunk.

> ABI (V.O.)
> I drank a lot. And one day...
> (swallows hard)
> ...you got sick. Really sick. I'd passed out.
> (voice cracks)
> You-you... you almost... died.

Pastor Lucas spies through the window, then rushes inside, shocked. The little boy trembles with fever and overwhelming fear, his face streaked from hours of crying. Empty beer and hard-liquor bottles lie on the floor.

INT. MOUNTAIN CABIN - NIGHT

> ABI
> But Pastor Lucas... He heard you crying.
> He broke in and took us to the hospital.
> (pause)
> You know, we were sitting there, in that
> little waiting room, waiting to see if you'd
> make it. And you know what he said? He

looked me straight in the eyes, into my soul, and he said, "The more knowledge, the more grief."

(shakes her head)

And I don't know... it was like... like he somehow knew what I was going through. Like he knew I had this big secret crushing me.

(wipes a tear)

Pastor Lucas is an angel, a saint. He saved you and me. He changed my life. Helped me find God. And God taught me how to care about you. Care on a real level, Bowie.

(soft smile)

And... you became my son. My Bo-Bo. God... You can't possibly know how much I've loved you ever since.

BOWEN

I love you too, Mom.

ABI

(voice breaking again)

But this world, Bowie...

(whispering)

It's not God's world.

(pause)

I used to think it was real. I believed in it, got pulled into it. Just like everyone else.

(pause)

But I know better now. And this isn't real, Bowie. It's not.

BOWEN

It feels real to me.

ABI

(crying, whispering)

What do you think happened to our souls?

BOWEN

Mom, what are you talking about? Your soul is still here. Right here. Stop talking like that.

(leans in)

Hey.

He holds her face, brushing away her tears, then angles himself to meet her eyes. She looks away, resisting. But finally lets him in.

BOWEN

Mom. C'mon. Don't you love me?

ABI

(hugging him tight)

Of course I love you. I love you more
than anything.

BOWEN

See? You still love. You still feel. I mean,
you even feel regret...

(soft smile)

Now tell me that's not a soul.

She gives a small smile. She looks torn, caught between
her faith and her reality. But something in her eyes softens,
as if hope is finally breaking through.

EXT. LOBA'S TREEHOUSE - TERRACE - DUSK

The sky burns orange above two miles of waterfalls
cascading down 300-foot cliffs. Mist rises from the deep,
green forested canyon, catching the dying light. The sheer
scale of the artificial beauty is breathtaking.

Sharing a laugh, the Möbius crew sits around a large
wooden table on the terrace. Dinner is finished, plates
scattered, wine flowing.

J.S. clenches his jaw, his black gaze penetrating Abi,
who sits opposite to him. The memory of the ambush, the
massacre of his friends, burns behind his eyes. Abi shrinks
under his stare, unable to look up. He leans in, unable to

help himself.

> J.S.
>
> So Akira...

> ABI
>
> Abigail. Please... call me Abigail. Or Abi.

She touches her crucifix necklace, feeling uncomfortable.

> J.S.
>
> Right. Sure. Abi... so you're not gonna try
> to kill us tonight, right?

V gives him a weak punch. *Not funny.* Abi forces a thin, polite smile, but her eyes drop to the table. The guilt is still there. Bowen watches her, worried. This might be too much for her. Too soon.

Bowen turns to Loba. She seems distant, her gaze fixed on the screen floating near the railing. It is broadcasting the news, its lower third reading, "Human Preservation Act results will be announced shortly."

> BOWEN
> (whispers to Loba)
> You nervous?

Loba shakes her head, pouring more red wine into an already full glass, the liquid trembling dangerously at the rim. She glances at J.S., her eyes narrowing slightly, then takes a long sip.

She stands and raises her glass to make a toast. She cringes, wrestling with her own words.

LOBA

You know, we were heading into very dark times.

(pause)

Rhea wasn't just gonna wipe *us* out. She was gonna rewire the minds of everyone else, robbing them of who they are.

(looks at J.S., then points to

Akira)

And she started with Abi.

J.S. exhales slowly, the rage draining out of him. He looks at the older woman and gives her a small nod.

LOBA

But now... Rhea will rot in prison. And the people finally know the truth. They believe us. I see the change already. Even the purists are starting to change their minds about us.

(turns to Bowen)

And what can I say? We wouldn't be here without you. Your conviction. Your tenacity.

BOWEN

It's okay. You can say "stubbornness."

They laugh. Abi opens her eyes and nods. *Tell me about it.*

LOBA

No, but seriously. The sacrifice you made. Thank you.

Bowen smiles and looks down, embarrassed by the praise. It seems impossible that just last week, he hated virtual reality. Now, here he is, an artificial man living in artificial worlds. Maybe even in love with an artificial woman?

LOBA

The United Worlds is finally free.
(showing her arms)
I get goosebumps just saying it out loud.
(raises glass higher)
So here's to that. To truth. To freedom. And...
(pause)
To the new United Worlds.

ALL

To the new United Worlds!

They clink glasses, the chime ringing out against the roar of the falls. Bowen nods at Loba, his eyes saying, *great speech.*

She shrugs and grimaces. *Not really, but who cares?*

Bowen turns to meet his mother's sweet eyes. She smiles and takes his hand. They've been through so much, but there's hope.

They settle back in, telling stories, laughing...

On the screen, the news anchor disappears, replaced by a countdown to reveal the Human Preservation Act results.

>10...
>
>9...

Loba shushes everyone. The laughter dies off.

>7...
>
>6...

Everyone holds their breath, eyes fixed on the countdown. No one moves.

>5...
>
>4...

The roar of the waterfalls pulses louder, filling the silence. The buzz of the cicadas rises in anticipation.

>3...
>
>2...
>
>1...

>CUT TO BLACK.

In the sudden darkness, the waterfalls continue to roar, louder and louder, while the scream of the cicadas rises into a deafening symphony.

The deep, guttural roars of howler monkeys echo like thunder.

Written by
BLASKI

CREDITS

Lucila Duloup	Cover & Illustration Artist, Book Designer
Anselm Kiefer	Painter of *Böhmen liegt am Meer*, 1996.
Al Horner	Reviewer of 3rd and 6th drafts
Juampi Rasore	Reviewer of 2nd draft
Ricky Luque	Reviewer of 1st draft
Lucila Duloup	Reviewer of all drafts
Stephanie Taylor	Copy Editor of 7th draft

If you enjoyed this experience, please consider leaving a review. Goodreads, Amazon, or wherever you can is great.

Feel free to message me if you want to talk about the book.

Thank you for reading United Worlds, and till next time.

@blaski.writer

blaski.writer@gmail.com

www.united-worlds.net

www.ingramcontent.com/pod-product-compliance
Lightning Source LLC
Chambersburg PA
CBHW020540120726
47903CB00001B/53